ADVENTURES OF A
BIRD-SHIT FOREIGNER

ADVENTURES OF A BIRD-SHIT FOREIGNER

SULAYMAN X

alyson books
NEW YORK

© 2006 BY SULAYMAN X. ALL RIGHTS RESERVED.

MANUFACTURED IN THE UNITED STATES OF AMERICA.

THIS TRADE PAPERBACK ORIGINAL IS PUBLISHED BY
ALYSON BOOKS, P.O. BOX 1253, OLD CHELSEA STATION,
NEW YORK, NEW YORK 10113-1251.

DISTRIBUTION IN THE UNITED KINGDOM BY
TURNAROUND PUBLISHER SERVICES LTD., UNIT 3,
OLYMPIA TRADING ESTATE, COBURG ROAD, WOOD GREEN,
LONDON N22 6TZ ENGLAND.

FIRST EDITION: SEPTEMBER 2006

06 07 08 09 10 **a** 10 9 8 7 6 5 4 3 2 1

ISBN 1-55583-982-7
ISBN-13 978-1-55583-982-6

BOOK DESIGN BY VICTOR MINGOVITS

A LIBRARY OF CONGRESS CATALOGING-IN-PUBLICATION DATA
APPLICATION IS ON FILE.

This one's for my mom,
because starting over is what we do best.

ONE

AT SOME POINT during the year 1983, a G.I. from Kansas City visited a prostitute in Bangkok, Thailand, while said G.I. was on R&R from "war games" being staged in the region. Said prostitute worked at a bar called Pussy Glory on the seedy set of alleys and streets known collectively as "Soi Cowboy." Famed for her "pussy-smoke-cigarette" acrobatics, said prostitute did a nightly show exhibiting same, entertaining offers from the endless stream of men that surged through Soi Cowboy looking for love or any semblance thereof. Lust, of course, was not to be sniffed at.

Having had one abortion too many, this prostitute, by the name of Nida, was advised by her doctor to carry her newly discovered pregnancy to term or risk almost certain death. Nida, exhausted by the pussy-smoke-cigarette show—not to mention using her vagina to open Coke bottles or shoot darts at balloons held by drunk male patrons—and in desperate need of a break from all this foolishness, agreed. Thus did a boy named Isa come into the world.

It had not occurred to the young woman that the father of the baby she was carrying might be a foreigner; most of her clients were Thai men, after all, and she had assumed that the baby would also be Thai. A horrible surprise awaited: The child was fair-skinned, almost white, with distinctly Asian features but very clearly a European or American father.

Nida was horrified beyond telling, as were her parents, relatives, and even the doctor who delivered the baby. She was horrified because it was generally assumed, though not quite true, that only prostitutes had sex with foreigners and only sentimental, sloppy prostitutes kept the offspring of such unions at hand. Goodness knew there had certainly been enough of such "half and halfs" left behind in the wake of the conflict in Vietnam. A whole generation of fatherless kids had been sired by heedless servicemen, kids who could not hide their racial background, who were assumed to be the offspring of whores and G.I.s and thus not really "Thai," though there wasn't anything else they could be.

Given that Thai society valued conformity as a social prerequisite, to not only step beyond the socially decent bounds of maintaining one's purity but also to have sex with a foreigner, then keep that offspring around as a constant reminder of one's sin—it was all very shocking and upsetting, a tremendous loss of face, both for the woman and her family.

Isa crawled his way out of his mother's womb and into this minefield completely unaware of what was to come, unless it was hinted at in such things as grimaces when he cried or rough hands when he was handled or the continuous absence of both his mother and his father as he grew up, and the refusal of his grandparents to say much concerning either.

The grandparents had a small banana plantation in a province quite distant from Bangkok. Isa grew up surrounded by banana trees and the workers who tended them and the snakes who made their homes within them and the ghosts and spirits who surrounded them. His grandfather was a tall, spare man given to whiskey and gambling, which kept the family in constant poverty. Whenever the grandmother had had enough of this nonsense, there were arguments and fights, which escalated into shouting, screaming and all sorts of violence as they hurled what few possessions they had at each other, with Isa often huddling in some corner hoping their wrath would not turn on him, though it very often did.

Isa's childhood was filled with year after year of ridicule and rejection from his grandparents on down because of his skin color. He could not hope to disguise it, came to despise it, to despise his body, his pale face, his white legs, everything that screamed out the fact that his father had been a foreigner and that he was just one more little bastard left behind by some man who had no idea what he had done or what it had led to.

The children at school were merciless: Isa was called "half-breed," "half and half" and "bird-shit foreigner," which meant he could not speak his own father's tongue, English, and that was certainly true. That said students were likewise at a loss with the Queen's tongue, well, what matter was that? Their parents were Thai, after all.

Teachers did not intervene in the torment dished out to Isa day after day, torment he tried to ignore or sometimes agreed with in the hopes of satisfying his tormenters enough to make them stop or sometimes violently disagreed with, storming off from the school premises to get away, to run back home, to lose himself in the banana plantation, with its comforting smells of banana trees and earth.

Neighbors and children in the village were no kinder. Isa was the butt of jokes, excluded, left out of games, refused even the most basic points of decency and kindness all because he was not like others. He was different, and to be different in a culture that values only conformity is to die daily. This particular rural, somewhat backward society had no use for bird shit foreigners.

Isa's only consolation was that his father—whoever that had been—had been white and not black. On the Thai scales of degradation, having a black father was just about as low as one could get. It ranked right down there with being Cambodian. This was small consolation, given the constant ridicule and rejection he faced at every turn and from every quarter. Yet it was indeed some consolation, one small thing to be proud of. It could have been worse.

In every society, of course, there is a class of those who are not wanted, who do not fit in, who cannot, who never will. They exist at the margins. They stand outside the windows looking in. Sometimes, like Isa, they stand at windows looking out, filled with restlessness because they know, down inside, that they don't belong where they are. They are mistakes, and they know it.

Isa was one of these unfortunate souls, and like all the rest, he would do his best to fit his squares into circles until the truth finally made itself known. Like all the others, he would feel like an alien from outer space, abandoned here on this confusing, wicked world, abandoned for reasons he would never understand. Like all the others, he would keep trying to be something he was not until he became exhausted from the effort. Then and only then would he become what he was. This is the story of how that happened.

TWO

ONE EVENING, AS the sun fell from the huge sky and the men returned from the depths of the banana plantation, Isa climbed a tree in the backyard so that he could have a good view of the open shower area. As they did every night, the men returned and went round the back of the house to the shower area and discarded their clothes to shower and clean up. It was the hot season, and after working all day they were covered with sweat and dust and took a good, long time to cool down. Isa watched these proceedings, a strange, excited feeling in his belly.

The shower area was fenced off on two sides, so it could not be seen from the house, but anyone else who was out and about could avail himself of the sight, if he so pleased. There were four large water jars, always full of water, with lots of large plastic bowls floating on top of the water, and the men stood around these jars, naked, dousing themselves with plastic bowls of water, shampooing their hair, soaping their bodies, laughing, and carrying on as they always did.

Isa stared at their naked bodies, his eyes greedy. Over the course of his fourteen years of life, Isa had often seen his grandparents showering in this fashion, and had never thought much of it. They were old, their skin wrinkled, altogether ugly. He showered himself there, and had never paid much attention to who might see him. Modesty was not exactly a virtue out in the boondocks.

From the house, he heard his grandmother calling. "Isa!" He glanced at the house nervously. Why was she calling him? The men paid no mind. "Isa!" she called again, her voice angry, impatient. He was going to have to get down from the tree to see what she wanted, but if he did so, the men would surely notice him, would surely wonder what he had been up to, whether he had been watching them, which, of course, he had.

She called again.

Frowning, Isa tried to quietly climb out of the tree, but one of the men, Chok, was watching him and offered a knowing sort of smile. Isa glanced at him, at the thick bit of flesh between his legs, and hurried off.

When his grandmother caught sight of him, she gave him some money and told him to run to the village and buy some cooking oil. Then she cuffed him on the back of the head and told him not keep her waiting next time she called.

THREE

SINCE SCHOOL WAS out, Isa had little else to do but make sure that he stayed out of everyone's way, so the next day he went out into the banana plantation, down the rows of banana trees, as far from his grandparents' house as he could get. After a half a mile or so, the banana trees came to an abrupt halt and jungle took over. The jungle was frightening, filled with spirits and who knew what else: snakes, tigers, large spiders, poisonous plants, maybe even wild elephants. It was not the place for a fourteen-year-old boy to play, so he didn't go into the jungle but rather walked along the edge of the plantation for a long time, the mysterious jungle just off to his left. The sun overhead was hot on his bare back, the earth hot beneath his feet.

He kept watch for snakes. He knew that the ones that slithered off quickly were not the ones to be afraid of. Rather, it was the dark snakes who wouldn't even get out of your way. Those were the ones who were poisonous, dangerous, not to be messed with. They were the sort that often lazed about in shady spots. Cobras were also poisonous, and, worse, they were chasers—if you angered one, it would come after you like a devil from hell—and they were fast, terribly fast. The best thing to do when a cobra was about was sneak off in the opposite direction, giving it as wide a berth as possible. Pythons were another story. Huge, sluggish pythons liked to hide and ambush. Isa was deathly afraid of pythons, had yet to see one that wasn't as long as he was tall, had nightmares about waking up at night and finding himself in a death grip, having the breath squeezed out of his body so that the python could eat him at its leisure. It was not unusual for pythons to be ten feet in length and much longer, and during the rainy season they were a constant source of terror because one could never tell whether they were swimming about in the vicinity during the frequent flooding, those who could tell usually found out the hard way.

While walking thus, minding his own business and hurting no one, he heard footsteps behind him. He turned around to see Chok coming through the trees, carrying a banana knife, a sort of machete that was used to cut banana clusters from the tops of the trees. There was a strange look in Chok's eyes and also a sort of smile.

"What are you doing, boy?" the man asked, squinting at Isa.

"Nothing," Isa said. "Just walking."

Chok looked over his shoulder, as if to see whether he had been followed. "You've been watching us, haven't you, half and half?"

Isa, feeling guilty, could only stare at the ground between them. Indeed he had been watching for a number of weeks now. Chok grabbed hold of Isa's shoulder, turned him around, and ordered him to walk into the jungle.

"Where are we going?" Isa asked, frightened. He did not want to go into the jungle, was afraid of snakes, was afraid of the spirits and ghosts.

"Never you mind," the man said, walking just behind him.

Isa pushed his way through the dense vegetation. They were quickly swallowed up by towering trees and enormous fronds. He heard the buzzing of mosquitoes and the rippling of leaves as the wind blew. It was altogether spooky. There was too much darkness and shadow for his liking.

They came to a clearing, of sorts, and the man stopped, grabbed Isa's shoulder and turned him around. "You see this?" he asked, holding the machete close to Isa's face so that he could not possibly do anything else but.

Isa nodded fearfully.

"You're going to help me do something," Chok said, "and if you don't, I'm going to take this banana knife and slit your throat. Am I making myself clear? Fucking slit your throat. You understand me, you little faggot?"

Trembling, Isa nodded.

"Take your shorts off, boy," the man said, his voice very quiet.

Take his shorts off?

"Do it," the man said menacingly, bringing up the machete for Isa to see, as if he meant to skewer him right then and there.

Isa pulled off his shorts. He felt confused, frightened.

"Your underwear, too," Chok said.

Isa took his underwear off.

Chok now looked him over, grinning to himself, letting his hands feel Isa's belly, back, his bare buttocks. "You're a pretty boy, aren't you? You like to look at us, don't you? Well, how does it feel to have someone looking at you, for a change? You liking it, half and half?"

Isa trembled, did not respond.

The man removed his own clothes, and Isa could see that

the man's penis was hard, poking at the air. He didn't want to stare at it but couldn't help himself. The sight of it was arousing, made something in his belly flutter.

"You like it, don't you?" the man asked, grinning. He pushed himself close, poking at Isa's belly with it. Isa stood there and did nothing, not knowing where this was going to lead, what it meant. "You know you like it, pretty boy. Now, why don't you turn around and kneel down and put your hands on the ground?"

Very slowly, Isa did.

The man knelt behind him, and Isa glanced over his shoulder, nervous, afraid, but also excited. But when the man began poking himself inside Isa's body, the pain of it was so intense that Isa could do no more than try to jerk away and make the man stop. The man would not. Instead, he pushed himself all the way inside and clutched at Isa's hips with strong hands, refusing to let him go.

"It hurts," Isa whispered fearfully, afraid someone, somewhere, would hear. He began to cry.

To say that it hurt was an understatement. It did much more than hurt. Isa thought the man might actually be killing him. The pain was so sharp, so vivid, so excruciating, he could hardly breathe. It felt like the man had stuffed the banana knife straight inside his arse and was twisting it around.

Chok did not answer, merely did his business, which he accomplished in about three minutes—three very painful minutes for Isa—before getting to his feet and leaving Isa to lie on the grass and shadow, panting, sobbing, bewildered.

"Don't you forget about this knife," Chok said, kicking him

in the leg to make sure he was listening. "You say a word about this to anyone, I'll cut your fucking throat and don't you think for a moment that I won't. You think anyone gives a shit what happens to you, half and half? Hah!"

FOUR

AFTER AWHILE, ISA sat up and looked around the clearing, suddenly frightened, suddenly realizing where he was and that he was naked and vulnerable. Something bad could happen if he continued to lie there and do nothing. A python could be stealing through the brush, ready to ambush. He put his underwear and shorts back on and got painfully to his feet, hobbling back the way he had come, through the large fronds, wanting to get out of the jungle before . . . whatever.

His butt and lower back hurt, and this made walking difficult, but he ignored the pain and hurried as fast as he could, not stopping until he reached the safety of the banana trees. From there, he walked slowly, in a sort of daze, uncertain as to what had just happened to him or what it meant.

When he got back to the house, he first went to the bathroom, sitting there for a long time, waiting for something to come out. Nothing did. Mystified, he eventually went to the bedroom and crawled onto his mat on the floor, where he fell asleep and had strange, troubled dreams.

FIVE

SONGKRAN, THE THAI New Year festival, was just around the corner. Would his mother come home and visit? The next day he was obsessed with this question.

"Can I call and ask her if she's coming?" he inquired of his grandmother.

"And waste our money?"

"I want to know if she's going to come to see me."

"Why would she want to?" his grandmother demanded. She was cooking breakfast, and he was pestering her.

"I miss her," he said.

She laughed at him. "What a baby you are. You miss her? She's lying on her back in some hotel with her legs spread and letting some foreigner get his jollies. What's to miss? She's a whore. Look at you, you're a bird-shit foreigner. She should have had an abortion, but the doctor told her she'd had too many already. You should be thankful to that doctor, you wouldn't be standing here today, if not for him. Why are you always under my feet?"

"Please, I want to call her," he said, desperately wanting to hear the sound of his mother's voice. He had not seen nor heard from her in years.

"I said no," his grandmother exclaimed, using a spatula to slap at the stovetop to emphasize her point. "Would you get out from under me and go do something?"

"Please, Grandma?"

"You're not wasting our money!" she snapped. "Just as well she stays away. Now get out of here and stop bothering me."

"Please, Grandma?"

"Goddammit, Half and half, I said git your ass out from under me! Now git!" She slapped the spatula on the stove again.

He went outside, frowning at the endless banana trees, thinking about his mother, wishing he could talk to her, hoping she would come and visit. But then, she never came to see him, did she? And she never called. What made him think it was going to be any different this year? How long had it been now? Four years? Five?

Thoughts of his mother led to thoughts of his father, and a keening grief seized him. Was there ever a man Isa hated so much yet loved so intensely? Hated, because the man had abandoned him or was perhaps not even aware of his existence; loved, because the man, whoever he was, was his father, and only one man in the whole world could claim such a thing. Where was his father? Why didn't his father come for him? Why had both his parents abandoned him?

The workers were arriving, congregating at the large carts used to ferry the banana clusters in from the depths of the plantation. From the carts the clusters would be loaded onto the old truck that Isa's grandfather drove, to be taken into town and sold at the market. He saw Chok among the workers, saw the man's eyes looking at him, saw something like a smile playing about on his large lips. The strong man walked over to where Isa was.

"At lunchtime, I'll expect to see you, same place," Chok said. He put his hand on the handle of the banana knife, now hanging from his hip, as if to emphasize his point.

"You be sure to be there, Half and half. You don't want no trouble, do you?"

Isa looked up at him, frightened.

"You understand me, Half and half?" the man asked.

Isa nodded. A cold dread settled into his belly.

SIX

AFTER BREAKFAST, HE went walking through the banana trees, staying well clear of the men, who were working down in the south end today. He stayed north. His thoughts wandered away from the subject of his mother and fixed themselves on a boy in the village named Som. Isa was in love with Som, as silly and stupid as that sounded. He should be in love with a girl, but he was not; he was in love with a boy. He could spend hours thinking about Som, about his handsome face, his white teeth, his strong body. He could spend hours thinking about what it would be like to play with Som, to be his friend, to be his brother, even, to be part of his family, to sleep in the same bed with him, to eat breakfast with him, to go to school with him, to be loved and respected by him.

He frequently daydreamed about being Som's little brother. How proudly he walked, in his daydreams, by Som's side, known to everyone as Som's little brother. How proud it made him feel! Nobody at school would laugh at him or call him a bird-shit foreigner, because if they did, Som would knock their heads in and make them very sorry indeed. After school, they would walk home together and then bathe together, both of them naked. They would even wash each other's hair. At night, they would sleep in the same bed, probably naked since it was so hot. He would lie next to Som, listening to the boy's breathing. He would watch the boy's bare chest rise and fall. He would feel the warmth of the boy beside him, all night long. Whenever he woke up, Som would be lying there, beautiful Som, naked Som, wonderful Som.

He rubbed at his face, these thoughts, these daydreams, making him both happy and sad: happy because they were so sweet and fun to have but sad because it was all untrue. Som was not his brother, would never be his brother. Som called him a bird-shit foreigner just like everyone else. Som did not want to be the friend of the son of a prostitute and some G.I. So, while he loved Som, he also hated him. They coexisted in his mind, this tender, affectionate love, this powerful, black hate. Som was the epitome of everything he desired, everything he could never have.

Som and his friends often went to the nearby river to swim in the mornings, so now Isa's feet took him in that direction. His grandparents' plantation was next to the one belonging to the Umbot family. If he cut through their plantation, he could get to the river, so he did, but cautiously, because the Umbots did not like kids playing about in their banana trees, not that the bananas were going to be disturbed by anything the kids did, but the Umbots were strange that way. So Isa darted from one tree to the next, paying careful attention so as not to come upon some of their men.

He found Som at the swimming hole with his friends Nat and Nui, who were brothers. Som was a year older than Isa, in the next grade at school. He was bigger than Isa, stronger, had all sorts of confidence in himself, his body, his abilities, his standing in the community. Isa caught sight of him, thought about how beautiful he looked, and there was a strange ache in his heart, as if that beauty was killing him, as if that beauty might make him physically ill.

When Som and the two brothers saw Isa emerge from the trees, they called to him. "If you want to swim with us, you know what you have to do," Nat yelled from the river where they were swimming. The boy was already grinning with anticipation.

Isa knew. Still, it was a small price to pay if they would let him swim with them.

He took off his clothes and waded into the river to join them, but they were in a hurry and quickly congregated around him. They were all naked—they had always gone skinny-dipping since ever Isa could remember—and Isa's appearance had made them horny. Now they wanted their blow jobs, the price Isa had to pay if he wanted to play with them. It had been that way for three years now, and Isa did not consider it to be unusual. They all stood around in waist-deep water while Isa did this, laughing amongst themselves, cuffing Isa on the back of the head, making lewd comments about how he was a faggot, a cocksucker, a lady boy, a bird-shit foreigner, about how they really ought to throw him on his hands and knees and fuck him like the dog he was. He did what was expected of him, staring up at Som fondly when it was Som's turn, taking the boy's hardness into his mouth with a feeling much like happiness in his breast, choking down the semen when it came—always too quickly, when it was Som—and offering not a word of complaint.

When they had each gotten what they had wanted, they waded out of the water and quickly got dressed.

"I thought you were going to swim," Isa said, feeling hurt.

"We're finished," Som said, laughing. "See you later, cocksucker."

They started to walk off, but Som stopped, turned around, and grabbed up Isa's shorts and underwear.

"No!" Isa called out, afraid they would run off with them.

They did.

He waded out of the water as quickly as he could, but they were too far ahead of him, and they were running out in the open. Isa couldn't go running after them, not when he had no clothes, not when they had such a head start.

He watched their departing backs, hating them now, hating Som especially, feeling humiliated and angry. There was nothing to be done but go home, so he darted back through the Umbot's plantation, doubly careful now, afraid he was going to be seen. How was he going to explain it? He eventually got home, grabbed a pair of shorts from the clothesline in the back of the house, and ran to the outdoor shower to put them on before anyone saw him. Then he sat down at the wooden table in the backyard and cried quietly into his hands.

SEVEN

AS LUNCHTIME APPROACHED, Isa remembered what Chok had said, and he felt frightened. What if the man wanted to bugger him again? The thought of it filled his belly with a strange terror. Blow jobs were one thing; Chok was something else entirely. Yet what choice did he have? When the man said he would slit Isa's throat, Isa believed him. The men who worked the plantation were rough, liable to do most anything and not think twice about it. If he didn't go, the man would be angry. Where could Isa hide? How could Isa manage to evade him? He could not. So, just before lunch, he walked through the trees, back to the spot where the man had found him the previous day.

He did not have to wait long for Chok to show up, and this time he was accompanied by another man, one of the other workers. They marched him into the jungle, each of the men taking a turn, and by the time they were finished, Isa was in terrible pain again. So it went, for the rest of the summer.

The Songkran Festival came and went. His mother did not call, did not visit. The attentions of Chok and his friends became worse: more hurtful, more frightening, more intense. By the end of the summer, five of the workers had discovered that Isa could be used in this fashion—used with impunity since he was too terrified to tell on them—so use him they did, usually in twos or threes. By summer's end, Isa was having nightmares every night. He even told his grandmother on them, and she laughed in his face and said he was a whore just like his mother and why the hell should she care about what they did to him? At least he was good for something.

He stopped going to the swimming hole, hating Som with all his fourteen-year-old heart, hating that arrogant sneer, hating the way Som used him. But then there were times when he sat around and thought about the blow jobs he'd given Som and how he would gladly give him more if he wanted them. He thought about how beautiful Som was, how happy it had made him feel to put his hands on the boy's hips and take the penis into his mouth while staring at the boy's brown belly and belly button and strong legs, and such thoughts left him filled with an unexplainable grief.

Sometimes he thought about sticking his head in one of the water jars and keeping it there until he was dead. Other times, he thought about using one of the banana knives and impaling himself on it, like the Japanese guys did in the movies. Sometimes he walked alone in the evening among the long rows of banana trees and cried, not knowing why he was crying, not knowing why he was in such pain, not knowing how to make it stop. And sometimes, at night, he thought about Som and couldn't stop himself from masturbating.

ONE

WHEN THE MONSOON rains came, Isa decided it was time to leave because there was no other option. He could not stay. He could not stand Chok and his friends, could not stand his grandparents. Most of all, he could not stand the thought of going back to school again and having to face all those hateful bastards who laughed at him and called him half and half and fag boy and cocksucker, and bird-shit foreigner. And anyway, he knew that he was not really wanted, that his grandparents tolerated him but nothing more, that they didn't really love him, not the way other kids were loved by their grandmas and grandpas.

One Sunday evening, he stole money from his grandfather's wallet to purchase a bus ticket to Bangkok, taking with him little more than a change of clothes as he hurried off into the night while his grandmother watched her favorite soap opera and his grandfather got drunk on cheap whiskey.

There was only one Bangkok-bound bus that came through the village, and it did so each evening at about eight P.M. Isa lied when the ticket seller asked him if he had his grandparents' permission to be going off on his own. He said he was going to visit his mother in Bangkok and would be returning in a week or so. With ticket in hand, he stood waiting, too anxious to sit down, terrified that someone would go tell his grandparents what he was doing, desperate for the bus to hurry up and arrive.

Eventually, it did. He boarded, feeling both frightened and excited, and before he could find an empty seat, the bus was moving, and his little village disappeared into the darkness behind.

It took five hours to get to Bangkok, and by the time he arrived, it was just after midnight and he was starved. He had no money for food, though, so he set off in search of Soi Cowboy, where his mother worked at a bar called Pussy Glory. He knew this because his grandmother never tired of telling him about his mother's sordid past, her job, her place of employment. His grandmother had often asked if Isa wanted to "end up in Pussy Glory," shorthand for being a failure like his mother. If he didn't do well at school, his grandmother would taunt him: *You want to end up in Pussy Glory, half and half? You going to sell your body like your mother because you're too stupid to do anything else?*

Of course, he had never seen the real Pussy Glory, wasn't quite certain what went on within its four walls, and did not even know what the words pussy and glory stood for since they were not Thai words.

From the Morchit bus terminal, he was told it was perhaps an hour's walk down the main thoroughfare—Sukhumvit—to the area known as Soi Cowboy, so he hoisted his small bag over his shoulder, stared at the crowds of vendors selling foods and sweet stuffs with greed in his eyes, and set off.

Bangkok was simply huge. The traffic was so thick and the exhaust fumes so overwhelming, that he tied his handkerchief over his face in a vain attempt to block out some of the dirty smell. He had walked no more than ten minutes before he began choking as the pollution got into his nose and throat.

Aside from that, it was thrilling. The buildings were so incredibly tall, and there were so many people out and about on the streets—so many vendors, foreigners, dogs, guys on motorcycles, guys on bikes, police officers, fortune-tellers—that sometimes every bit of space on the sidewalk was crowded with vendors and customers and dogs and he had to walk in the street itself to continue on his way, despite it being past midnight. Yet, for a boy with no money in his pocket, it was not too terribly exciting. And when he looked at the way folks were dressed and then compared their dress to his own tank top and shorts and plastic flip-flops, he felt a keen sense of shame and embarrassment.

When he finally found Soi Cowboy, he walked around, in a bit of a daze given all the gaudy lights and loose women. He eventually found Pussy Glory and was suddenly terrified. Several scantily clad women were sitting on bar stools by the front door, their legs crossed, cigarettes perched between fingers, makeup just a bit too heavy. Above their heads was a neon sign, flashing on and off: Pussy Glory. Pussy Glory. Pussy Glory.

"Ain't you a bit young?" one of them asked.

"Ain't he just the sweetest thing?" another said, giggling.

"You looking for love, baby?" the first woman asked. "I got lots. I could scoop you up in a minute and eat you piece by piece, you're such a sweet-looking thing."

The women giggled with this.

Isa blushed. "I'm looking for my mother," he said, struggling to make himself heard over the din of disco music and the noise of the street. Somehow the thought of these women eating him made his skin crawl.

"He's looking for his mother!" the first woman exclaimed. "Imagine that. Sure you got the right place, baby? I could be your mother, if you want. You wanting to breast-feed?"

This produced more giggles and more embarrassment for Isa, who was beginning to question the wisdom of his decision to come here. He had no idea what his mother would say to his just appearing on her doorstep. She would most likely be mad. Yet he desperately wanted to see her.

"What's her name, baby?" another asked.

"Nida," Isa answered.

The women exchanged looks. "We don't have anyone working here by that name, sweetie," one of them said.

"She's my mother," Isa said, shouting to be heard.

"But no one by that name works here," the woman replied.

He made a hurt face; he had not expected this. "Where did she go?"

More looks went around.

"Just a minute," the first woman said, getting to her feet. "You sure she's your mother? You're not just wasting my time? Her name's Nida?"

Isa nodded.

The woman disappeared into the bar.

While he waited, Isa took in the street scene: dozens of bars and go-go joints, women sitting outside each establishment shouting to the men who walked by, trying to get customers to come inside, to have a "good time." Disco and dance music blared here and there, but rock and roll too: Aerosmith, the Eagles, even some Ike and Tina from the 1960s. Isa had never heard any of this music, much less heard it played so loud, and thought he must have descended into one of the hell worlds of Mara, such a dreadful din it was.

The women took to him, playful, suggestive, but he could tell they were not necessarily serious. After his initial embarrassment, he began to like their attentions. No one had ever called him "baby" or "sweet thing." It was heaven to his ears, to hear himself called "sweetie" and "darling" and "loverboy" and "cutie pie."

Isa was, in fact, completely unaware of how beautiful he was. His looks were indeed a curse but a blessing, too, perhaps the one weapon he'd been given by the gods. His hair, a light brown, fell in wondrous disarray about his forehead and neck; his lips were full, the sort one can't refrain from looking at and thinking about; his body, while thin, was well proportioned; and he was filling out nicely, especially in the chest and buttocks. His skin was pale, with just a touch of soft brown. But his eyes were his most attractive feature, somewhere between gray and green; in a world where only brown eyes were to be seen, they were utterly striking.

"Who's your new boyfriend?" a man called to the women jokingly from the street.

The women paraded themselves around Isa, pouting, hamming it up, talking about how they were going to teach this boy a thing or two that he would never forget. Eventually, the first woman returned with the man who owned the bar. "Your mother's not here any more," the man said loudly.

"Where did she go?" Isa asked, feeling a sudden, strange urge to cry.

"She went with some foreigner. To Europe. Denmark. I don't know. She quit. She doesn't work here any more."

Europe? Denmark?

"I need to talk to her," he exclaimed. "I don't have anywhere to stay. I came to see her."

The man shrugged helplessly.

"When did she leave?" Isa asked.

"Two years, three years?" the man replied. He shrugged, made an apologetic face.

"But I don't have anywhere to stay," Isa said again.

"Your mother doesn't work here any more, kid," the man said before he turned around and disappeared back into the bar.

Isa began to cry, putting his face in his hands, quite upset now, not knowing what to do. It had not occurred to him that his mother might have left her job, much less that she had gone off to Europe with some foreigner. He did not want to think about what that meant: that she would leave him behind, that he was of no importance to her. Which, of course, was precisely the truth.

"What is it, baby?" the first woman said.

"I don't have anywhere to stay," he mumbled through his tears. "I came to see her. I haven't seen her for almost four years now."

"I'm sorry, baby," the woman said, holding him and patting his head. She could see what was obvious: Isa was a half and half, the child of a prostitute and some foreigner left to fend for himself.

"Look, kid," she said kindly, "you can't stay here. You've got to go now. This ain't a place for kids. Why don't you go hang out by Lumphini Park; you'll find some homeless boys there. They'll take care of you, tell you what to do. I'll give you some money. You hear me? Lumphini Park – that's where you should go."

She dug several one-hundred-baht notes out of her bra and handed them to him.

"Now, you go on," she said gently. "Take care of yourself."

He looked at her, wiped his eyes, and turned away, going back into the streets from whence he had come.

TWO

ISA WALKED AWAY from the Soi Cowboy area, his appetite gone, tears streaming down his cheeks, which he wiped at absently, clutching the money he'd been given tightly in his fist lest someone try to steal it from him. The money—

five hundred baht—was more than he'd ever had in his life, certainly more than the eighty baht he'd stolen to get this far. He could use that money now to turn around and go back home. He could walk back to the bus terminal, purchase a ticket, repay his grandfather the money he had stolen, keep the extra for himself.

No. He would not do that. He didn't know just precisely what he was going to do, but he knew he wasn't going to go back, not now, not ever. He would rather die of starvation than go back.

He walked, aimlessly, not knowing where Lumphini Park was, too upset to ask someone. All of it was overwhelming. The lights, the towering buildings, the throngs of people, the ugly dogs in the streets and on the sidewalks, the vendors and their wares, the constant noise of the traffic, the fumes, the smell—it was like he'd stepped off the banana plantation into the midst of hell. There was nowhere to sit down, no benches, no chairs, no toilets, just endless concrete and gaudy lights in every direction: backward, forward, up, and down. It made his head spin.

He walked farther down Sukhumvit, through a huge intersection—he had to race across it, dodging cars that would not stop for him—and past more buildings, skyscrapers, crowded sidewalks, restaurants and bars, go-go clubs. He continued to wipe at his eyes, feeling miserable, frightened, lost.

An older boy appeared at his elbow. "Where you going, *Nong*?" the boy asked, using the affectionate word for "younger brother."

Isa glanced at him, suspicious. The older boy had bloodshot eyes, seemed a bit dirty, a bit strung out. He shrugged, not knowing what else to do or say.

"Why are you crying?" the older boy asked.

Isa shrugged again.

"You need someone to help you?"

Isa didn't answer, just kept walking, frightened by this older boy, wishing he would go away.

"Come on, *Nong*, I'll help you," the boy said agreeably, putting his hand on Isa's shoulder in a friendly gesture, as if to say, You see, there's nothing to worry about; I'm as friendly as can be.

They walked in silence for a couple of minutes through the midst of another set of vendors. Once past them, the street cleared, and Isa found himself mostly alone with the other boy. He paused, stopping to look at a display window at a travel agency, not wanting to continue on alone with the other boy, afraid of him, wanting to turn around and go back to where there were some people and safety.

The pictures of planes and city skylines reminded him of his mother, and he felt a fresh wave of tears wanting to fall from his eyes, but he resisted them. Where the hell was Denmark anyway?

"What's the matter, *Nong*?" the older boy asked.

Isa shrugged.

"You got any money, *Nong*?" the older boy asked, a bit aggressively.

Isa glanced at him, fear in his eyes.

"Give me your money, *Nong*. Give me your money or

I'll fucking kill you." The older boy backed him up to the window now, his face turning ugly with hate. Isa opened his fist, showed the older boy the money. He was trembling with fear. The boy grabbed it, stuffed it in his pocket. Then, with a swiftness that surprised Isa, he backhanded him and then kneed him in the stomach, making him double over and fall to the sidewalk in sudden, surprise agony. He was then given a kick to the stomach that sent him sprawling face down on the concrete in horrible pain.

The boy ran off before Isa could so much as open his eyes and see what direction he'd gone off in.

THREE

HE ASKED FOR directions to Lumphini Park and walked there. The sun was already up by the time he arrived, the gates open, so he went inside and began to walk around, glad to see trees and flowers and grass and wide-open spaces, glad to find a public bathroom where he sat on a toilet for the best part of thirty minutes, glad to have a contained, quiet place to sit and not be looked at.

Leaving the bathrooms, he found a bench, sat down, clasped his hands in his lap. Why hadn't he just walked back to the bus terminal and gone home after the woman had given him that money? Now he had no money. Nowhere to go. Now he couldn't go back, even if he wanted to.

Of course it was all his fault. As his grandmother never tired of pointing out, Isa had bad karma, had done something bad—terribly, horribly bad—in a past life, and now he was paying for it, and paying through the teeth. If he suffered, it was just, it was fair, because it was the result of what he'd done in his previous life. He was not to expect any sympathy from his grandmother or anyone else. He'd been born a half and half as punishment for his sins. His lot in life was to accept this and shut his mouth and endure the suffering. If he did, he could, perhaps, hope for a better rebirth in his next life. But if he whined and complained about it, then he would only make it worse for himself, and who knew what sort of horrible rebirth he would have the next time around. He might even be born as a Cambodian. What could be worse?

So, as Isa sat there in the park, he was not feeling sorry for himself. He was thinking that it was all his fault, that his karma was bad, that he was paying for his past sins, that there was no injustice to any of it. If Chok and his friends had dragged him off into the jungle and raped him, it was because Isa had done something in a previous life to deserve it. If his grandmother slapped him or spoke rudely to him or threw things at him, it was his fault; she was simply helping him burn off the effects of his bad karma. If he was rejected and ridiculed by friends, it was only right, because he was low born and deserved rejection and ridicule. In some strange way, the people who hated him and made fun of him were actually helping him; they were making sure that he paid for his sins so that he could have a better rebirth in his next life. It was only proper that he be grateful to them. Even the fact that he was attracted to men was his own fault; it meant that he had committed adultery in his previous life or had been a bad wife to a good husband.

That this whole business was an insane perversion of what the Lord Buddha had taught concerning the matter of karma did not occur to him. That its purpose was to keep low-class people in their place so that the rich and mighty could continue to exploit and lord it over them was not something his fourteen-year-old mind was capable of wrapping itself around. He knew only what he'd been told: He had bad karma. He was suffering for his sins. He deserved what he got. It was nobody's fault but his own if life had dealt him such a pitiful hand. He was not to whine about it, because that would only make it worse.

Exhausted, his belly aching for food—why hadn't he thought to eat when he had had money in his hand?—he lay down on the bench and fell asleep.

FOUR

HE WOKE UP at some point in the afternoon to find several boys standing around the bench, staring at him, poking at him, trying to get him to wake up.

He sat up, startled, sudden fear in his belly.

"What are you doing, *Nong*?" one of the boys asked. This one seemed to be the oldest, maybe sixteen or so. He had an ugly face and long, dirty hair.

"Nothing," Isa said.

"Well, why don't you go do 'nothing' somewhere else, you fucking half-breed?"

Isa made to get up, but this boy pushed him back down. "Just kidding, half and half. You new?"

Isa stared fearfully at him, shrugged.

"He's new," one of the other boys said. "We would have seen him before by now if he wasn't. Probably from fucking Isan or something." Isan was in the northeast of the country, its poorest area.

"You hungry, half and half?" the oldest boy asked.

Isa nodded.

"If I give you some food, will you suck my dick?"

Isa made a face, embarrassed by the question, by the fact that it had been asked of him.

The boy laughed. "Give Half and half some food," he ordered.

Isa was handed a small plastic bag full of sticky rice, which was cold and perhaps a day old, if not more. He did not care. He ripped off a hunk of it and stuck in his mouth.

"What's your name, half and half?" the first boy asked.

"Isa."

"Isa? What a fucking dorky name. We'll just call you Half and Half, you know, like that, with capital letters. That'll be your name: Half and Half. What do you think of that, Half and Half?"

Isa gulped down more of the sticky rice and shrugged. He was reminded by the boy's remarks that his name was Isa because his mother, on the way to the hospital to deliver him, saw a sign stating that "-isa and Mastercard" were "accepted here," that his name was a small joke.

"If you don't hang out with us," the boy continued, "you

can't stay in this park. We'll fucking kill you. But if you hang out with us, you'll be alright. Okay? You got it? And I'm the boss. You do what I say; you'll be alright. You got it, Half and Half?"

Isa nodded.

"Now, since you're new, you've got to suck me, so come on."

Isa's arm was grabbed by one of the boys, and he was dragged to his feet and made to follow as the leader of this little gang walked off the beaten, concrete paths of Lumphini Park and into the darkness and privacy of the trees. They came to a secluded place where, if the others gathered around and kept an eye out, Isa could kneel down on the ground and suck the leader's penis. Which he did.

He did it because he had no choice, because he could not fight all of them, and because he needed to make friends with someone, anyone. He needed food, a place to sleep. He needed someone to tell him what to do and how to survive. He needed companionship. So he knelt down and sucked the boy's dick. He ignored the way they sneered at him and made jokes about his being a half and half faggot.

"You must have done this before," the leader said. "Don't even have to tell you to watch it with the teeth; you're a real cocksucker, aren't you? Probably like it, don't you, Half and Half? You're just a little fag-boy, aren't you?"

Isa, of course, could not respond to this.

"Yeah, you suck that real good, fag-boy."

After another increasingly frantic minute, Isa choked back the semen that squirted into the back of his throat, trying not to gag on it, grateful when the boy finally pulled away and zipped up his pants.

When this was finished, he needed something to drink, and someone handed him a bottle of water. Someone else handed him a plastic bag. He stared at it, somewhat stupidly.

"You're supposed to sniff it, Half and Half," one of the boys said. This boy seemed closer in age to Isa and had delicate, almost feminine features. "My name's Chai. You ever sniff glue before?"

Isa had not.

The boy demonstrated. Isa did as he was told, sniffing the glue, surprised when the rush hit his brain and made him feel slightly euphoric and sick.

They now introduced themselves. The leader's name was Gong. The other boys were Chai, Nit, Uon, and Sombat. They all sat down, gathered around the tree, passing around the water bottle, sniffing glue, passing the time, bonding. Isa did not need to be told that each of these boys had also "sucked" off their leader and were in his shoes at one point, and probably not too long ago. At any rate, that was how Isa's life of crime began: sucking a smelly, teenage dick, then being taught how to sniff glue.

FIVE

THAT EVENING THEY left the park because it was closing and no one was allowed to remain inside it at night. They did not go far, though. Isa was told that each corner of the park was frequented by certain sorts of people looking to buy certain sorts of sex. Prostitutes hung out on one corner, faggots on another, underage boys—like themselves—on another, and so on.

So he found himself hanging around with Gong and the others, waiting to be "picked up" apparently someone would come along and want to have sex with him, would pay him. Then he was supposed to come back here and give one hundred baht to Gong and keep whatever else remained. In return, Gong would take care of him. Gong would make sure he had food to eat, protection, glue to sniff, whiskey if he wanted it, drugs, whatever. Gong, in other words, was a pimp, and Isa was the latest addition to his stable of underage whores. Isa did not know this, of course, and did not know precisely where his association with this fellow was going to lead.

Gong made Isa hang back, by the fence and watch the others. As the night wore on, the other boys were picked up, one by one, mostly by old men.

"Now, when it's your turn," Gong said, "you just go with the man, do what he wants, and come back here. That's all. Give me my money, everything's cool. I'll take care of you, Half and Half. Okay? You've got nothing to worry about now; you're with me. Someone gives you trouble, I'll fucking rearrange his face. You just give me my money, and once in a while you suck my dick, and we'll be cool. We'll get along fine together. I like my boys to suck my dick . . . makes me feel good, you know? Not that I'm a fucking homo or anything. I just like it. And when I want you to suck it, then you got to suck it, and that's the way it is. You keep me happy; I'll keep you happy. Now, when the man comes along, you just go with him, do what he wants, come back here, give me my money. Simple, huh?"

Isa nodded.

Gong now sent him out toward the street where he could be seen, and Isa waited for someone to come along, feeling frightened, yet feeling better now about his chances of survival. Gong would take care of him. He would have friends to hang out with, friends who knew how to survive. Everything was going to be all right. So he waited, and eventually an old man came along and struck up a conversation and soon asked if Isa felt like going over to his house and "having something to drink." Isa complied, following the man, terrified, too inexperienced to ask for money up front, uncertain as to the outcome of this venture.

Once at the house, Isa was enticed into the bedroom, where his clothes were roughly removed and the pleasures of his flesh roughly taken in a lengthy and somewhat brutal and yet somehow dismissive rape, almost as if to say it mattered little how much Isa got hurt because there wasn't a thing Isa could do about it, which was precisely the truth. The man, when he was finished, gave Isa two hundred baht and told him to get out of his house.

Isa put his clothes on, took the money, and left. He returned to the park, where he found Gong waiting for him. He gave the older boy one hundred baht, and Gong smiled at him. "You're all right, Half and Half. You're a good kid. I'll take care of you, you hear me? Don't you worry about a thing. You keep the rest of that money and do what you want with it."

Isa put the other hundred-baht note in his pocket and smiled. For some reason, Gong's approval made him proud of himself. Isa had never received approval before, not from his grandparents, not from his peers, and certainly not from any older boy. To hear it now, to see the respect in Gong's eyes, was very satisfying indeed.

Gong gave him an affectionate, encouraging hug, rubbing playfully at Isa's butt, kissing the side of Isa's face.

"Now, you go back out there," Gong said, nodding to the street and pushing him away. "On a good night, you can do five, six, seven guys. So you get busy, Half and Half; the night is young." So Half and Half, strangely happy, got busy.

SIX

NIGHT AFTER NIGHT, horny men took advantage of him and deposited hundred-baht notes in his hand in exchange for his services. He would be taken to their homes or to a hotel room or to a bathroom in a bar or to an alley or even to a parking lot or behind a tree. He would give blow jobs or have his pants pulled down and his backside violated. Sometimes the men wanted to give *him* a blow job, and the only thing he was expected to do was lie back and enjoy it. Sometimes they wanted to take pictures of him while he was naked or masturbating or maybe having sex with one of the other boys. Sometimes the old men couldn't even get it up; they just wanted to talk. Sometimes they could get it up, but couldn't get it off, and it would take an hour or more of being sodomized before they could finish. After a while, it didn't seem to matter any more; it didn't hurt, and he didn't care what they did, as long as they paid, as long as the money kept flowing.

He learned to hustle, and he was a good student. And after every hustle, he returned to the park and gave Gong his one-hundred-baht payment, and Gong raked in the money hand over fist. With five boys going, doing about an average of five tricks per night, he was making about two thousand five hundred baht daily. He used this money to buy food and whiskey and glue bags and harder drugs, too, like heroin. Gong knew that if he kept his boys hooked on something like heroin, they would keep working for him and would soon forget about the unfairness of having to pay him each time they turned a trick.

Isa took to injecting heroin with gusto. He loved the way it made him feel. He loved being high. He came back from his tricks and gave Gong all his money and said he could care less about it as long as he could get high, as long as Gong kept up a steady supply of needles and white powder and a spoon to heat it up in.

Gong encouraged this addiction, was pleased to see it, pleased to see how eager this stupid boy from the provinces so willingly gave himself over to being used and abused and taken advantage of.

Isa learned that shooting up or popping pills like Ecstasy could kill pain, could make you feel good or make you feel nothing at all. He learned that if you drank enough whiskey before being fucked by a particularly large penis, you wouldn't feel a thing, that if a john was drunk enough you could usually filch money from his pockets without his noticing. He learned how to fight off crabs, how to steal candy bars and packs of cigarettes from convenience stores, fruits and sweets from unwary vendors. All these things Isa learned, as so many had before him, because he was not yet aware of his own existence. He looked in the mirror and saw eyes with dark bags beneath them looking haggard and old, not a beautiful young man with the blush of eternity upon his cheeks. One year passed in this fashion, and Isa turned fifteen.

>}<

---------- ONE ----------

THE MASTER WAS an old man with a beard and a white prayer hat by the name of Sheik Ahmad Kloy. He wore strange white robes. His and Isa's paths crossed in this fashion: Isa, having been taken by a heavyset, bearded man to the outskirts of Bangkok, found himself, at roughly three in the morning, terribly strung out on heroin and unceremoniously escorted to a front door after having rendered services requested and received funds for same. Paranoid from the drug, which he had taken too much of, he wandered down the steps and into the darkness, convinced something was out there, something that wanted to attack and destroy him. It began to rain. Clothed in nothing more but jeans and a vest—dressed like the whore that he was—he was quickly soaked to the skin.

The city had begun to take its toll: the pollution, the drugs, the smoking, his addictions, his poor diet—all of it was coming to a head, and Isa was ripe for a serious breakdown. On that particular night, the breakdown began.

He needed to get back to Gong. That was all he could think about. Gong always knew how to get him to come down. Gong always took care of him when he got strung out, but he couldn't remember where he was now, couldn't make out the names of the unfamiliar streets because the signs were swimming in front of his eyes, and it was raining too. Soaking wet, shaking from the sudden cold, he cast about for a place to take refuge, crawling into the first quiet place he could find, which, as it turned out, was the front of a mosque.

In the darkness and pouring rain, and in his condition, he paid no attention to exactly where he was, finding only that the recessed steps of the mosque's front door offered a quiet, out-of-the-way place where he could lie down. He began to feel very cold and very tired. The thunderstorm continued unabated. He had the thought that he should hail a taxi and get himself back to the park, back to Gong, but the thought drifted away, and thinking itself became impossible. Before long he fell into a fitful sleep.

The Master, who rose just before dawn each day to lead the early morning prayers at the nearby mosque, with his two youngest sons in tow, came upon Isa a few hours later, after the rain had subsided and just before the sun would begin to rise.

Aside from the jeans, the boy wore a leather vest that was open to expose his painfully thin ribs and chest and the more than abundant needle marks on the insides of his arms. His hair was greasy and unwashed though it appeared that some attempt at personal hygiene had been made. Gold earrings did not go unnoticed. The strings on his scuffed shoes were untied. The boy was shivering, and though his eyes were open, he did not seem to be aware of what was going on. It was an altogether pitiful sight.

The Master's oldest son, Hamid, sneered in disgust, muttering the word trash.

"Who is it, Papa?" asked his youngest, Abdul, who had just turned eleven and who knew little of the ways of the world, and who had not yet had time, like Hamid, to develop genuine prejudices.

The Master shook his head. "I don't know."

The Master recognized what he saw immediately, of course, and where others would see only sin and flagrant disregard for morality, his eyes beheld a soul in pain, desperately in need of healing, even love. For reasons that he had long ago given up trying to fathom, he understood, instinctively, that a new opportunity had been laid—literally—at his doorstep: the opportunity to love. And while some may prattle, others do, and the Master was one of the few in the latter category.

"Help me," he said to his sons, bending to rouse the boy.

"And do what with him?" demanded Hamid, suspicious, knowing full well his father's propensity for kindness to strangers.

"Care for him, of course," his father answered.

Isa was led away, his mind fogged and uncomprehending. The Master took him to his own house, installed him in a bedroom with instructions to his wife to care for the boy until he returned from prayers.

And so it began.

TWO

ISA SLEPT FOR the rest of that day and on into the night before coming to his senses. He woke in a darkened room, found himself lying on a mat on the floor, covered with a soft blanket. The sound of traffic could be heard through the open windows, but it was faint and far away. A fan blew warm air on his skin. In the corner of the room a small lamp was burning.

Feeling disoriented, he pulled the blanket around his bare body, looking about for his clothes. He thought perhaps he was in a trick's house unattended, that perhaps the trick had gone out or gone to work or something, and that it would be best for him to leave. But, flat on his back, he found he could hardly move that his forehead was feverish, his lips parched and hollow ache had settled itself in the base of his skull.

Then the Master came.

The Master was old, but there was a timelessness about his face, especially his eyes, which seemed to see all there was to see and much more besides. His beard was long and white and neatly trimmed, and his hands were strong but kind.

"Don't be alarmed," the Master said. His voice was like music, rich, soothing, pleasing.

"He should leave," the oldest son said. "Who wants this

kaffir, half and half trash in our house? What are my friends going to say?"

Isa did not know that a *kaffir* was an unbeliever, but he gathered, from the vehemence of the Arabic word when it was spoken, that it was not a good thing to be.

The father made a small shooing gesture with his hand. "In my house," the Master said, addressing himself to the older boy, "we offer kindness to strangers and help to those in distress, or have you forgotten?"

"He's an unbeliever!" the boy exclaimed.

"He's sick," the father replied calmly.

"*Take not unbelievers as friends!*" the boy said forcefully, quoting from the Koran.

"*Care for those who are ill, the traveler, the orphan*," the father shot back. "You dare quote the Holy Book to me in defense of your unkindness? Have I not taught you any better than that? You should be ashamed."

"You taught me to stay away from *kaffir* trash, to keep myself pure before Allah."

"And does that mean you remove yourself from the world you live in and refuse an act of kindness to one in need?"

The older boy was furious but said nothing.

"Forgive my son," the Master said, turning to address Isa. "Are you comfortable?"

Then, turning away, he spoke to his wife, saying the boy still had a fever and needed more of the medicine he'd prepared earlier. The woman turned to the youth standing in the door and bade him to fetch it, which he did but not before offering a disgusted sigh and an exaggerated rolling of his eyes.

Isa was peripherally aware of all these things but not completely so, for he was in a state of such disorientation and illness he could hardly think. But what he did know, and comprehend and understand was the love and kindness he saw in the Master's eyes and the gentle way the man's fingers touched his forehead or his cheek. He understood these things in the way that only those who have been denied them can: Despite his condition, the feel of the man's hand on his cheek was nothing short of miraculous.

But as soon as Isa recognized that it was love the Master had in his eyes, he grew afraid and uncertain. Love could be withdrawn. Love could crucify. Love was the rack he had stretched himself out upon for his absent father, pining for this man who would never know what he had left behind, yearning and aching for the feel of him, the smell of him, the strength of him, the sound of his voice, yearning and aching and desiring and needing but never satisfied. Love, too, was the rack he had been tortured upon for his mother's sake: How many were the days he had spent hoping she might call him or visit or come home for good? How many holidays came and went without her putting in an appearance? Now she had gone off to Europe. How much evidence did he need to know that she did not care for him? Love, love and more love he had given her, but like a dog that is continuously beaten by its master, the love had stopped, and the hatred had begun. Love was what he had given to Som, and what had he gotten in return? Love was not to be trusted. Love, at least as far as Isa's experience of it was concerned, was the most painful and bitter thing there was, and he wanted nothing to do with it.

He was trembling all over and had enough wits to know that it was drugs he needed, chemicals to calm the body, potions to soothe and caress and bring forgetfulness, but try as he might, he could not get up. His body simply wouldn't let him. He needed to get back to Gong; Gong would take care of him. Gong would know what to do. Yet, he had a mad thought, lying there: that he would like to be the Master's son, that he would like such a man as that for a father, someone upright, someone strong, someone close to the gods. Who would dare make fun of him when such a man was his father?

Then, there it was, that sharp, keening grief, that blade that twisted in his heart: How he longed for a father! The thought of it was enough to make his eyes sting with unwanted tears. To be held in his father's strong arms, to lay his head against his father's chest, to be told he was loved, to give up the struggle and rely on a powerful, kind man to provide, to put food in his stomach and clothes on his back, to teach him and protect him and show him the way in which he should go—what he wouldn't do for such things! A silent sob escaped him.

 Often in his youth he had laid in bed long into the night dreaming of such a man, inventing elaborate stories in his head, creating a world that was more real than the one he inhabited. Always he was the son of a powerful king. Always he played out the scene in which this powerful king roamed the countryside and finally happened upon the young boy who had been snatched away at birth, the young boy who was his son. The young boy was living a wretched life as a slave, totally unaware of his real lineage, lending his back to the hauling of rocks or felling of trees or digging of trenches, dirtied, uncouth, both his spirit and heart broken. Then the king would come and the likeness between them would be so obvious that the king would spirit him away to the distant grand palace where he would be bathed by an army of servants, where his hair would be trimmed and fashioned and his body clothed in fine materials before he was presented before the royal court amid a joyous celebration. The king's son had come home!

Over and over that scene had played itself out in his mind, and each time it became more real, more substantial, more sweet than anything in the world. In such a fantasy world there was no pain, no grief, no devils to trouble and torment him. But it was just like his fantasies about Som—and just as unreal—because the truth was, Isa did not belong. He was one of those souls who stood outside windows, looking in, filled with unquenchable longings. Isa was a mistake, an unexpected consequence of promiscuity that had to be tolerated until it was old enough to go away and exist on its own without causing any further trouble.

He sobbed. He did not know why. He knew only that he was in pain, that there was something dark and hurtful in his breast and that there was something in the Master's eyes that had thrown him completely off balance, that had made him remember all these things he had been desperately trying to forget.

THREE

OF HEIGHT AND stature, the Master was average. His graying hair was closely cropped but his beard allowed to grow, though kept neatly trimmed. His eyes were a soft brown. On his head was a white prayer hat, and he was clothed, most days, in white muslin robes. Of faith, he was a Muslim, long associated with a Sufi order to satisfy his more mystical bent. Culturally, a Thai Muslim man who ran his own business—a small restaurant serving Muslim food to an appreciative clientele—he also served as the prayer leader, or Imam, for the local neighborhood mosque, a task entrusted to him because of his piety and learning.

The Master cannot be understood without reference to his being a Sufi, but to understand a Sufi, one must get into the mind, into the bloodstream, the guts, thoughts, dreams, and desires of the subject, for Sufism is tied up with these things and cannot be understood apart from them. Islam is a strong religion, the religion of the One God: *There is No God But God! And Muhammad is His Prophet!*

It demands submission and rejects anything but complete monotheism. To associate partners with God is most abhorrent. It will not do. It is *shirk*, heresy, error. Everything is laid out for the believer: what you may do, what you may not. The terms are clear and stark: Paradise, for those obey and do the right; *Gehenna*, for the unbelievers. It is a strong religion, and this strength is also its weakness. It is possible to feel overwhelmed by Allah, terrified into submission, but that which is terrified rarely loves truly and honestly, and deeds motivated by fear are worthless deeds, unworthy of the majesty of God. Hence, Sufism.

To a Sufi, Allah is the Beloved, the goal, the destination, the best thing one could achieve. To annihilate oneself into the Beloved is all that a Sufi desires. *There is No God But God* means that nothing is worthy of the human heart that is apart from God, nothing worth desiring that will detract from God, nothing worth having that is not God, nothing that can be worshipped except God. Money, fortune, name, power, prestige, material goods—these are nothing compared to the Beloved. They are unworthy substitutes for one's worship. The Sufi makes it his business to love Allah, to love the Beloved, to be consumed in the Beloved's mysteries. In return, the Beloved instructs His disciples and uses them to bring healing, hope, and happiness to the troubled world.

The Master, now approaching fifty years of age, had been devoted to the Beloved since his early twenties. Each day he led the *Salat*, the daily prayers, at the mosque where he was the Imam, where he had been such for more than a decade. For the Master, there was no god but God, and there was nothing worth achieving or doing that was not done for the sake of the Beloved. In the course of his training he had learned to rely on his heart and his gut, through which the Beloved often spoke. If he felt a mood, an impulse, a prompting, he paid careful attention, for in these things the Beloved spoke, and frequently.

The Master had learned his lessons well and knew that Love forgave all, Love was patient with all, Love conquered all, Love bent all to its will. Love did not judge nor condemn.

The business of Love was to heal. It was not for foolish ends that the Beloved had created mankind. No, indeed not. It was for noble ends, for noble objectives. Thus, when the Master had come across the figure of a youth sprawled on the steps of his mosque, he had read the signs correctly: The youth had been led there because he was in need. It was the Beloved taking care of His own, for had not the Beloved created this boy? And as a servant and slave of the Beloved, it was the Master's duty to do as the Beloved wished, no matter what his family or associates might think of it.

FOUR

THE MASTER'S WIFE went to the garden in the back of the house where the Master was seated, deep in meditation.

"He is resting," she said.

He could detect the resistance in her voice, the undertone that said she disapproved, that she did not want some *kaffir* in her home, that she feared the effect the boy would have on their two youngest sons who still lived with them. Bad enough to be a street kid but to be on drugs—heroin of all things, what with all those needle marks on his arms and legs—oh no, she did not want any of that, not in her house. The Master understood all this from that tone in her voice.

"How can the boy be anything but a *kaffir* if we do not reach out, if we do not share what Allah has taught us and given us?" he asked.

The wife made no reply to this, merely bowed her head and went about her business.

FIVE

ONLY SLOWLY DID Isa become aware of himself. He was horribly ill, that much he knew.

There were voices saying things he could not understand. There were hands, touches, medicine, cool cloths, fresh bedding, long periods of silence, joints and bones that ached, eyes that would not open, eyes that opened but saw nothing. There was endless vomiting and dry heaves. There was shaking, trembling. Pain upon pain, unpleasantness—he felt like rats had gotten inside his body and were chewing away at his insides.

Then, at some point, he was sitting up in bed, most of his pain gone, drinking from a mug held by the Master. The taste of the drink was pungent, bitter, but the Master forced it down, encouraging him to drink every bit of it. A boy stood to one side, younger than Isa, holding a towel and washcloth. Another boy, the hateful older one, carried in a large basin of water, placing it on the floor next to the mat on which Isa lay, turning his dark gaze on him.

When Isa had finished the drink, he lay back, feeling disoriented, thoughts trying to form but unable to. The liquid burned his throat, moved down to his stomach, and spread out, feeling like a fire, making the room seem suddenly hot. Then the Master was dabbing at him with a cloth, wiping his face, his forehead, smoothing back his hair, wiping underneath his jaw, across his lips, the feel of it delightful. The younger boy knelt and pulled back the covers, removing them entirely. Isa could feel their hands going to work, wiping at his body, cleansing him, rinsing the cloths in the basin, not speaking.

The older boy took hold of one arm, and ran his cloth over it, pausing to gaze at the needle marks in the crux of the elbow, frowning. "There are so many," the boy said.

"Love is big enough," the father answered.

"I hope you're right," the son replied.

Isa did not connect these words with the tracks on his arm. He understood the words, but the words themselves had no meaning, no context to fit in to. He felt incredibly tired, exhausted, weak, and made no complaint over anything that was done to him. All he really wanted to do was sleep.

SIX

WHEN HE WOKE next, he could see faint light streaming into a window off to his right. He gazed at the window, perplexed. Where was he? He felt much stronger, and tried to sit up, letting the cover fall away from his skin. Beside him, on a mat similar to his own, lay the older boy, dark hair tousled in sleep, bare back outlined in the morning light.

He could not remember where he had been or how he had come to be where he was now or even where he was at all. He attempted to stand, to find his clothes, to leave, but almost as soon as he stood, he fell over, his legs seemingly without strength of any kind, and as he fell, he made a noise that woke the older boy, who flew out of his sleep and got to his feet instantly.

"Hey!" the boy said excitedly and fearfully, pushing Isa back to the mat, hands fumbling for the cover. "You're not going anywhere just yet."

Isa, head now wracked with pain, could not even bring himself to respond. He took many deep breaths, and when the pain began to subside, he opened his eyes to see the older boy standing there, in loose shorts that clung to his hips, regarding him with a suspicious eye.

"You stay where you are," the older boy said in a menacing, frightened tone. Then he disappeared out of the room and quickly returned with the Master following him.

"I must leave," Isa said. He had to get back to the park, back to Gong, who would be furious with him for leaving, for being away for such a long time.

"You must rest," the Master countered, pushing him back down on the mat, urging him to lie still. Isa did not protest. There was something about the Master's touch that would not allow him to. "You are very sick," the Master said. "When you are feeling better, you may leave, if you choose. We mean you no harm."

Isa was lost in the music of the man's voice, in the gentleness of his presence. This was a man who could walk into a room and command its attention without uttering a word.

"Who are you?" Isa asked quietly.

"Indeed," the Master said. "I am Sheik Ahmad Kloy. You may call me 'Papa,' if you wish; I have six sons already." And with that he laughed gently and touched Isa's cheek. "What's one more, eh?"

Isa smiled at this, taken in by the man's kind demeanor.

"I must leave," Isa said again. "I don't belong here."

"And who does?" the Master asked, shrugging his shoulders.

"I have to get back to Gong," Isa said.

"You need to rest and take care of yourself," the man replied.

"Gong will be furious with me."

"You must rest. Surely he'll understand. You've not been well."

The Master's wife came into the room, bearing a tray with a steaming mug of tea, which she set carefully on the floor beside the Master. The old man stirred it, watching it with some interest, lifting it to his nose to sniff it. "More medicine for you," he said, when the drink had cooled, glancing at Isa and smiling. Isa sat up and drank as much as he could. It was that same bitter, pungent drink that set his insides on fire. Almost immediately he felt drowsy and fell asleep.

SEVEN

AND SO IT went, for many a day and night.

Isa had been lodged in the "boys' room," a bedroom shared by Hamid, the older, and Abdul, the younger. The boys were both tall, Hamid more so, thick of frame, and heavy with muscle. Abdul was the opposite, the younger boy's waist small, his limbs like sticks. Both were dark-haired and had white teeth that flashed in easy smiles. Their beds were mats on the floor, with matching blankets and pillows, all of which were picked up and stored away daily. Each boy had a desk and a wardrobe. The walls were decorated with soccer posters and little else. It was on the floor of the room that these two youths shared that Isa found himself. A third mat had been installed just for him.

Almost two weeks into this peculiar arrangement, Isa's thoughts finally came back to him, and he began to comprehend his situation. He could sit up easily and take food from the tray on his own. The pain was gone, but the tiredness and fatigue lingered. When he needed to, he could make his way to the bathroom down the hall and take care of his business by himself. He could even shower. But how long could he stay?

He wanted to go back to Gong . . . but why? He wanted more heroin . . . but why? And anyway, it was sweet to spend his days resting and being cared for by this strange family. No one had ever cared for him like this. His grandmother certainly hadn't. No one had ever bathed him, or spoon-fed him, or mixed special medicines for him. No one had ever touched him with the love that he felt in the Master's hand. No one had ever looked at him the way the Master did. Who was this strange old man? What did he want?

EIGHT

"WHAT IS TO be done with you?" the Master asked one evening after sending his two sons away. "That is the question I have been asking myself. What is to be done?"

"I must go, of course," Isa said hurriedly, afraid that his welcome had worn thin.

"That is not what I meant," the Master said. Carefully the old man sat down, bringing his legs together, putting his hands on his knees, regarding Isa intently. "You may go, if you choose, but would you consider staying? And anyway, I suspect you don't have anywhere to go to. Do you?"

Isa took his gaze away from the man and did not speak.

"If not, you may stay here until such time as you are ready."

Isa did not reply to this either, and the man did not speak any further, only sat gazing at the boy, who, he noted, was painfully white of skin, brown hair too long, spilling about his forehead and down to his shoulders. The shoulders themselves were too thin, as were the arms and legs, as though there were no strength in them. The belly was pinched, as though it had not had enough to eat in ages. The boy was, in fact, altogether pathetic. There was none of the health and vitality so essential to the demands of youth, of growing bones and expanding muscles, no easiness of movement and lightness of heart, no curiosity, no irrepressible need to laugh and make merry. Only heaviness, thinness, an unhealthy pallor on the skin, eyes that looked at you with such despair and suspicion and fear. The Master felt a heaviness grip his heart, and he thought, *Is this how a child of the Beloved should live? Is this how a child of the Beloved should be treated? How can this be?*

Such thoughts, he knew, led directly to a place he did not wish to go: questioning Allah. The temptation was insidious, easy to give in to, easy to entertain, to let play upon the mind, to let enter the mind and the thoughts and the heart until it could not be pushed away. He refused it.

Allah has reasons for all that He does, and it is not for a mere man to question. Are there souls in the world seemingly abandoned by Allah, left in misery and darkness and suffering? If so, then any slave of Allah must take responsibility for it and get to work. Why curse the darkness when there are candles to be lit? So the Master stared at the boy and smiled and thought about what the future might hold for the two of them.

>4<

ONE

THE NEXT MORNING was Saturday, and when Isa woke, he felt fully himself for the first time in weeks. He did not rise right away. He lingered on the cusp of wakefulness, letting dream imagery slip through his mind, becoming slowly aware of the light streaming in from the window, the sounds of breathing—Hamid and Abdul lay next to him—basking in the sensations of health restored, a mind at rest, a body that no longer hurt.

He sat up slowly. Hamid and Abdul were at some distance away, lying next to each other. Abdul was completely covered, but Hamid had thrown the blankets back, and his back was exposed. It was a strong back, full of power, muscle, manhood. But Isa remembered Hamid's hateful words and mean looks and felt dispirited. There was a fist in that glove, a thorn in that particular rose.

The room itself, he saw, was quite old. Wallpaper was

threatening to peel, paint on the windows was chipping, the windows themselves, though washed, had gone beyond the age when mere soap and water could keep them new-looking. The desks and wardrobes were brown wood, old, modest, solid but not pretentious. Everything about the room showed care, usefulness, utility. There was nothing wasteful, nothing extravagant.

He looked about for clothing but could find none of his own, so he stood slowly, naked, and walked across the room, finding a pair of Hamid's shorts, which he put on hurriedly. They were very loose on his waist, but he paid this no mind. Glancing out the window, he saw gardens and trees. A dog barked. It seemed unusually quiet, at least for a city the size of Bangkok . . . if he was still in Bangkok. He looked out the window, saw skyscrapers and huge apartment buildings in the distance, was reassured.

He walked around slowly, gazing about the room, taking in the details, before making his way out into the quiet of the house. In the bathroom, he did his business, wishing there was a toothbrush he could use but not daring to use one belonging to someone else. He stared at his face in the old mirror above the sink for a very long time as he used a finger to rub toothpaste against his teeth.

When he went back out into the hall, Hamid was standing there, staring at him.

"Are you better now?" the boy asked.

Isa shrugged. He was afraid of this boy, did not like his hateful looks.

The boy watched him uncertainly, as if he didn't know

what to say or do. "You're wearing my shorts."

"I'm sorry," Isa said.

"You don't have to apologize."

Isa lowered his eyes.

"Are you a heroin addict?" the boy asked.

Isa didn't lift his eyes to look at him. Was he a heroin addict? What sort of question was that? He had never thought of himself in such terms, it had never occurred to him to do so.

"Why don't you go lie down?" the boy suggested, something in his voice sounding a bit unnerved.

Isa went back to the bedroom and lay down. The other boy followed, sat down on the floor and gazed at him. "Are you a Muslim?" Isa shook his head. "Then why do you have a Muslim name?"

Isa could only shrug. He did not know his name was a Muslim name. Isa was just a stupid name, a joke his mother played, just one more thing to be ridiculed over.

"You *do* know who Isa is, don't you?" Hamid asked.

Isa shook his head.

"Isa? The Prophet Isa? His mother, Mary? His father, Joseph? The Christians call him Jesus? You don't know any of this?"

Isa shook his head. He knew nothing of religion.

"You must be really stupid," the boy said.

Isa closed his eyes and did not respond. At that moment, he felt very stupid indeed.

"I didn't mean it like that," Hamid said, seeing the look on Isa's face. "Anyway, are you feeling better now?"

Isa nodded, not looking at him, still smarting from the insult.

"I'll get you some clothes," Hamid said, trying to soften his tone. "It's about time for breakfast."

TWO

DRESSED IN HAMID'S clothes, he followed the older boy through the large house to the kitchen, where Mrs. Kloy had breakfast waiting. The Master was sitting at the table and smiled warmly at Isa as he urged him to sit down.

Isa was very hungry—the smell of food made him realize that—yet he was very self-conscious, nervous, uncertain of himself.

"Where's your brother?" Mrs. Kloy asked, giving Hamid a frown.

"Still sleeping."

"Wake him up."

Hamid rolled his eyes and left the kitchen, leaving Isa to stare nervously at the Master and Mrs. Kloy.

"Sit," the Master said, motioning to the chair just to his right. "Are you feeling better?"

Isa shrugged and sat down in the chair. He would not look at the Master. For some reason, he was afraid. He did not see the look and the frown that passed from the Master's wife to the Master himself.

"Are you hungry?" the Master asked.

Isa nodded.

"That's good," the man said agreeably.

Still, Isa would not look at him, could not bring himself to raise his eyes. Mrs. Kloy put food on the plate in front of him: fish cakes with rice, and a bit of rice soup, too, in a hot bowl. Isa picked up his fork and began to eat, but the Master reached over and touched his arm. "Can you wait, for just a moment?" the man asked in a curious voice.

Embarrassed, Isa put his fork down.

"Normally, we thank Allah for our food before we begin eating," the man said, as if explaining himself. "We'll pray when the boys come."

Isa stared at the food, his face red.

"We should always thank Allah for everything, shouldn't we?" the man asked, as if making conversation.

Isa shrugged. He did not know who "Allah" was or why he should be thanked for anything.

The boys took their places, as did Mrs. Kloy. The Master said something in Arabic, to which the family replied, in Arabic, all of it meaningless to Isa, all of it strange and unexpected.

Then the Master picked up his fork and began eating. "Go ahead," the man said, urging Isa to eat.

"Are you a half and half?" Abdul asked straight away, his young face screwed up in curiosity.

"Abdul!" Mrs. Kloy said angrily.

"I'm just asking," Abdul said. "That's what everyone says."

"How impolite of you!" Mrs. Kloy exclaimed.

"Well, look at him, Ma," Abdul said, making his situation worse. "He's not Thai, that's for sure."

Isa felt ashamed and bit at his lip, for some strange reason wanting to burst into tears. He stood up and turned away, not wanting any of them to see his face.

"Where are you going?" Mrs. Kloy demanded in that same, angry voice.

Isa shrugged, wouldn't look at her, but was too frightened by her tone to go any farther.

"You need to eat," she said, more agreeably.

"You've offended him," Hamid said. "You're such a dork."

"I was just asking!" Abdul exclaimed.

"You're so stupid," Hamid said.

"Boys, please," the Master said. "Isa, sit down. Let's eat. Abdul, mind your manners. What's wrong with you?"

The boy frowned.

Isa sat down, his appetite suddenly gone, feeling very nervous and upset and unsure of himself.

"Probably smoked too much crack," Abdul said quietly, offering a naughty grin.

"Would you stop it?" Hamid said.

"Well, look at him!"

"You don't even know what crack is, you moron."

"Everyone says he's a crackhead."

The Master put aside his fork and spoon and sat back in his chair, regarding Abdul with a long, somewhat unfriendly gaze.

The younger boy shut up, recognizing that gaze and what it meant: His cheekiness was not appreciated, not at the moment, not when a stranger was sitting at their table. He ought to know better.

Then the Master turned to look at Isa, touching his arm again. "They're curious," the man said in a quiet voice. "That's all. Don't let them offend you. You don't have to answer any of their questions."

"What do you mean, 'their' questions?" Hamid demanded. "I didn't ask him any questions."

At least not in front of his parents, Isa thought.

The Master did not respond.

"I'm not a crack addict," Isa said, now raising his eyes to look at the younger boy, who was no longer grinning. "I was on heroin."

This was met with silence.

Now that the young boy had his answer, he seemed to have lost his steam.

"Are you happy now?" Hamid asked, rolling his eyes.

"Don't you have a mom and dad?" Abdul asked innocently, ignoring his older brother.

This question caught Isa off guard. Of course he had a mom and dad. Didn't he?

Isa tried to answer, but instead burst into tears. He got up again, and this time he did leave, hurrying back through the unfamiliar rooms, to the bedroom, where he shut the door so that he could cry without them looking at him, feeling so completely wretched he couldn't stand it.

After a minute, the door opened, and Hamid appeared, carrying Isa's food, which he placed on the floor and then sat down next to. Isa, lying on his mat, ignored the boy, hoped he would go away.

He would not. "Why don't you eat?" Hamid suggested.

Isa was trying to quiet himself, choking back his tears, feeling stupid and embarrassed and bewildered.

"Come on," the boy urged. "My brother's a dork. Don't listen to him."

Isa did not reply and eventually the boy got up and left.

He cried quietly for a long time before the tears tapered off, and afterward he remained where he was, hungry but not wanting to eat. He needed to get away from this house and these people, needed to get back to the park, to Gong, to the way his life used to be.

The door opened again, and this time it was the Master. The man crouched down, putting his hand on Isa's shoulder. "Why don't you eat? You'll never get better if you don't eat. Got to get your strength back."

Isa sat up, wiping at his eyes, feeling more comfortable with the man than he did with his sons. The man moved the plate and bowl closer, handing the spoon and fork to him. He ate but wouldn't lift his eyes to look at the man. When he was finished, he felt incredibly tired, and the Master urged him to go back to sleep. Within two minutes, he did.

THREE

THE EVENING MEAL went a bit more smoothly, perhaps because two additional youths were at the table: Muhammad and Bilal, nineteen and twenty, respectively, two of the Master's older sons who no longer lived at home. Yet, given that it was Thursday, the sons had come home for a family dinner.

"What's so special about Thursday?" Isa asked, when the others began to eat. Mrs. Kloy had prepared chicken with masaman curry, evidently a favorite with her husband and sons.

"Don't be stupid," Abdul said, rolling his eyes.

"He doesn't know about our ways," Muhammad replied, giving his youngest brother an impatient, shut-your-stupid-mouth look. Then, turning to Isa, he said, "Friday is our holy day. We don't work on Friday. We like to have a family dinner on Thursday. Tomorrow we'll all go to prayers together. We'll have to find a *kurta* for you to wear."

"Oh," Isa said.

"Doesn't Hamid have one his size?" Muhammad asked, turning to Mrs. Kloy.

Mrs. Kloy lowered her eyes rather pointedly, as if the thought of Isa wearing anyone's kurta was one she did not wish to entertain.

"Why does he have to wear mine?" Hamid asked.

"Because you're about the same size," the Master said, "and until we can get one made for him, you'll have to share."

"He'll look stupid in a *kurta*," Abdul offered.

Isa had no idea what a *kurta* was or why he would have to wear one.

"He'll look handsome, like a proper Muslim boy," the Master replied. "Aren't you capable of saying anything nice, Abdul, or do we have to have another talk about your tongue?"

"Oh, Papa," Abdul replied, rolling his eyes.

"If you could learn to control your tongue, the battle would be won," the Master said, in a way that suggested this wasn't the first time. "Anyway, it might be time for you to have another time-out."

"Papa!"

"Well, watch your tongue, then."

Abdul made a face but said nothing.

Before Isa had a chance to inquire as to what a *kurta* was and what was so bad about a time-out, the conversation moved on to the goings-on of the two oldest boys, who were now married and had kids of their own, and whom Isa would see on the following day at noon prayers. The members of the family gossiped, as families do, and Isa was unable to follow any train of thought since he knew nothing of these people or their personal history together.

With so many voices competing to speak Isa remained silent, and went unnoticed, which suited him perfectly well. He was glad for the food, glad of its warm, slightly spicy taste. He noticed that Mrs. Kloy would not look at him, had the sense that his presence was being tolerated by her but nothing more. The others, though, did not seem to mind his presence one bit. In fact, his presence had been noted, and they had moved on. Isa and his secrets were no longer of interest. He was now part of their orbit, if only on the cusp. There was a feeling that soon he would be included more fully.

Muhammad and Bilal spent the night, and thus there were five mats put down on the floor of the boy's room, all in a row. Isa was given the mat on the far left. Muhammad laid down next to him but said not a word. The older boy merely closed his eyes and went to sleep. They all did. Only Isa was left to stare up at the dark ceiling and wonder what the future might hold.

FOUR

ON THE FOLLOWING day he discovered that a *kurta* was an Islamic garment worn by boys and men. It was a sort of oversized shirt, with loose-fitting pants that were secured with a drawstring. The *kurta* he was given was white and fit him very well. To this was added a *kufi*, a prayer hat, also white. When he looked at himself in the mirror, he was surprised by how these clothes transformed him. First, he looked like the other Kloy boys, and this secretly pleased him. It made him feel as though he belonged. Second, he looked, well, different, like someone new. He was no longer Isa the heroin-addict boy-whore. He was Isa, the Muslim boy. This, too, was enormously pleasing, and he could not stop smiling at one and all.

That the other boys had changed in front of him, had shown him their bare skin, their intimate body parts, their naked butts and dark penises, had not escaped his attention. Of course they did not know that Isa was a money boy, was used to having sex with men, used to giving blow jobs. They simply assumed he was normal, like any other boy, and were not shy about dressing in front of him, as if the thought that he could be attracted to them sexually was so outrageous it could not even occur to them.

This pleased him too. He did not want to be reminded of his past, of the things he had done, of what he had allowed others to do to and with his body. He did not want to think about the men and their penises and their strange needs and moods. He did not want to recall the many times he had been on his knees before them or in front of them. He wanted to be the new person he saw staring back at him in the mirror. This new person was clean, pure, a new creation, a new being.

Dressed, as he was, from head to toe in white, it was hard to tell that he was a half and half. The white of the garments made his skin look somewhat darker. He might pass for a Southern Thai, known to look a bit different because of Malay roots. His face and hands, tanned by too much time spent in the sun, were just as brown as anyone else's. Only his strange gray-green eyes would give him away.

As they were preparing to leave the house, Muhammad looked over Isa's *kurta*, making sure that it was put on properly. Muhammad was tall and spare of frame, had kind eyes, and looked very much like his father. If Isa remembered correctly, the boy was at university studying to be a lawyer. He lived at the dormitory but came home on weekends, as did Bilal.

"How handsome you are now," Muhammad said, offering a grin. "The girls will be crazy about you."

Isa said nothing to this.

"Have you been to prayers before?"

Isa shook his head.

"Then stay next to me, and do what I do. Okay? Afterward, we'll introduce you to some of our friends."

"Do you think I look stupid?" Isa asked.

"Of course not," Muhammad said, frowning. "You look just fine. You've even got a Muslim name. Just do what I do, and everyone will think you're just visiting, a relative from the South, or something."

Reassured, Isa followed the older boy through the large house, which was far larger than any house Isa had ever lived in. Most of its windows offered views of trees and green, growing things. On the porch, Isa saw that he was in the main house of a housing compound, surrounded by gardens and orchards, with a road in the front leading to a gate that led out to the city beyond.

"My oldest brother lives over there," Muhammad said, pointing to a small house deeper inside the complex. "His name is Ahmad. He's married; they're expecting their fourth child any day now."

"Oh," Isa said. "And what about your other brother?"

"Sulay?"

Isa nodded.

"We might see him at prayers."

The subject seemed to be a sore one, and Muhammad would offer nothing further.

Isa wondered how he was going to keep all the names straight: Hamid, Abdul, Muhammad, Bilal, Sulayman aka "Sulay," Mr. and Mrs. Kloy—it was going to be difficult.

The others now appeared on the porch, and they were ready to go. Isa followed somewhat timidly and yet excited. There were three vehicles parked in front of the gate—two trucks and an old Honda—but they were not driving: the mosque was but three blocks away. They went through the front gate, which formed the end of a dead-end street, Isa saw. Townhouses rose up on either side, and the street itself was full of parked cars and vendors. How different the world looked! The street seemed absolutely vibrant, bursting with life and color. A scab-covered dog seemed to smile at Isa. The sun felt wonderfully hot and pleasant.

The Kloy boys, made a small parade of sorts, all dressed in *kurtas* and *kufis*, looking very Islamic and very cheerful, following in the wake of their parents. There were numerous other Muslims in the community, and the Kloy boys were apparently known to one and all, and many greetings were exchanged as they dodged potholes and vendors on their way to the mosque. The smells of chicken—fried, boiled, barbecued on outdoor grills—made Isa faintly hungry, yet he was too excited to be hungry. They passed small restaurants—always the ground floor of a three- or four-story walk-up town house—and Isa noticed that many of the men wore prayer hats and *kurtas*, that the women were at least veiled, if not covered completely from head to toe. Some had signs on the front of their shops in a strange language. When Isa inquired about a particular one, Muhammad said it was Arabic.

"What does it say?" Isa asked, innocently.

"Grilled chicken for sale!" Muhammad replied, offering a hearty smile.

In the light of day, Isa saw that the mosque was quite large, much larger than he had thought. He could barely remember how he had wound up lying on its recessed steps. The mosque was white, but the color was dingy, in need of repainting. Huge spirals marched up toward the sky. On the very highest one was the symbol of the sliver moon beneath the sun, the symbol of Islam.

The steps led up to double doors. Once beyond these, there was a large area for the depositing of shoes. The interior of the mosque was itself straight ahead. To the left were washing basins for the women, to the right, similar open faucets for men. Isa followed the Kloy brothers as they took over two of these faucets. There was a marble bench in front of each one, enough for two to squeeze on, and now Abdul and Hamid did just that, each going through what seemed to Isa a very complicated process of washing their faces, hands, arms, and feet. Numerous men and boys were doing likewise. There were about ten such faucets in a small semicircle.

Muhammad urged Isa to sit down next to him, and he explained what the process was all about and how it was done. "We have to perform ablutions before we pray," Muhammad said. "You start with your face. Just do what I do."

Muhammad first rinsed his hands, then scooped up water, rinsing off his face. Isa did the same. Muhammad then wiped wet hands through his hair rinsed out his nose and mouth did a very thorough job of hands and arms and elbows, then continued on downward to wash and rinse off his feet. Isa followed along as best he could, not understanding the seriousness of ablutions but determined not to inadvertently cause offense.

"Why are we doing this?" he whispered, leaning close to Muhammad, enjoying the feeling of the older boy so close to him; it made him feel safe, protected, secure, as though he belonged, that no harm could come to him.

"When we pray to Allah, we must be clean," Muhammad replied.

Isa accepted this in silence. They got up to make room for Bilal to do his ablutions.

Inside the mosque, the boys went straight to the front and took places in the front row. As they were the Imam's sons, this was expected of them. There, Isa was introduced, albeit quietly, to the oldest brother, Ahmad, who had his oldest son with him, a four-year-old boy. Yet there was a seriousness about the place that was not conducive to conversation, so Isa greeted the man quietly, then sat down between Muhammad and Hamid, waiting for the prayers to begin.

Over the past few weeks, Isa had heard, from time to time, a strange sort of voice calling out in the neighborhood. It wasn't the usual vendor driving by and advertising the prices of his goods over a loudspeaker attached to the top of his truck: "Clump of bananas, twenty baht!" Neither was it the politicians, driving by in trucks and giving speeches. Nor was it music blasting from an electronics shop. It was a sort of sing-songy chant, in a strange tongue, a sort of music that Isa had never before heard. Every now and again, as he had lay on the floor in the boy's room, he had heard that voice calling out but had never thought to ask anyone what it was.

Now that voice was calling out again, but it was extremely loud, so loud, it made him start. The voice was being amplified by speakers, and the interior and exterior of the mosque, were filled with it.

"What is that?" Isa whispered to Muhammad.

Muhammad bent close, putting an arm around Isa's shoulders, putting his lips close to Isa's ear. "That's the Call to Prayer. Whenever you hear that, it means it's time to pray. We pray five times a day. Didn't you know that?"

Isa shook his head.

"Well, now you do," Muhammad said, smiling.

With Muhammad's arm around him, Isa felt even better, even more secure.

There was nothing sexual in that touch, nothing that betrayed any sort of interest in Isa's body or sexuality. It was simply a brotherly, friendly thing to do. Thai boys frequently held hands. Even Thai men did so. It meant nothing more than friendship. Isa was too experienced now in the ways of the world not to sense the difference, though he wouldn't have been able to properly explain it to anyone who might ask. He just knew that Muhammad's arm around him meant that Muhammad thought of him as a friend, a younger brother. This in turn meant that Isa was to look up to Muhammad as an older brother figure, as was the Thai way. That, in turn, meant Muhammad was obligated to take care of him, should anything go wrong, or any problem arise. That was how it worked. From the king himself, all the way down to one's little brother or sister, it was patronage, plain and simple.

Hamid, sitting cross-legged on Isa's other side, gave off no such friendly vibes. Isa was aware that he made Hamid uncomfortable. Since that was so, why had Hamid purposefully sat next to him? Why did Hamid keep glancing at him? Why was there a certain sort of look in Hamid's eyes that made Isa faintly nervous? What was it about that look?

Wasn't it a hungry sort of look? A frightened, but fascinated sort of look? Wasn't there something sexual in it? All that Isa knew was that Hamid looked at him strangely. There was desire in his eyes but fear and even a bit of loathing, too, as if he were afraid of Isa.

The mosque quickly filled up with men; the women, he was told, prayed in a separate room where they could not be seen at all. The Master had spent this time out in the courtyard talking to various men, but as the mosque filled up, he walked slowly to the front, standing in front of his sons, ready to begin the prayers.

Isa followed along as best he could, but it was confusing. The prayers were in Arabic, so he had no idea of what was being said. It was like being at the temple while the Buddhist monks chanted in Pali: on and on, but what could it possibly mean, who could tell? Surely not Isa. They made a variety of movements. They bent forward at the waist, putting their hands on their knees. They knelt down, touching their foreheads to the floor. They sat back on their heels. They stood up. Knelt down. Prostrated. Isa kept his eyes on Muhammad, following his every gesture, hoping he wasn't making himself look like a fool. At one point, the Master got up and gave a short sermon. He discussed how the real jihad was to struggle with oneself, with one's lower nature, with one's inclination to sin and disobedience. More prayers followed this, and eventually Isa was led out to the courtyard and introduced to several Muslim boys, each of whom gave him a curious once-over with their eyes. This football game got underway.

By the time he returned "home," he was exhausted but happy.

FIVE

THE NEXT DAY was a Saturday, and Isa, feeling more himself than ever, went out to the gardens to help Hamid and Abdul pull weeds after Mrs. Kloy had fed them rice soup for breakfast. As it was the middle of the rainy season, the ground was muddy, making it easy to pull the weeds but making it impossible to stay clean. In no time at all, Isa was muddied up to his knees, and thanks to swipes at his face with muddy hands, he looked more like a farmer than a former boy whore. Not knowing that he had mud on his face, Isa was puzzled when Hamid, working in the row next to him, glanced at him and began to laugh.

"What?" Isa asked.

Abdul, attracted by this conversation, also glanced at Isa and burst out laughing.

"What?" Isa demanded again, feeling hurt.

The two brothers looked at each other, smiled, agreed that nothing was wrong, not a single thing in the world, and then they burst into laughter again.

"Have it your way," Isa said, frowning and grabbing for more weeds, trying to ignore them.

"It's a new fashion," Hamid said to Abdul.

"I saw it in *Elle* already," Abdul agreed.

More laughter.

Isa ignored them, his feelings hurt. He felt excluded, laughed at, embarrassed.

"I'll do you," Hamid said, going over to his little brother, doing something to the younger boy that Isa could not see because Hamid's body was in the way.

They whispered secretively, Hamid glancing over his shoulder to make sure Isa was watching them, offering a knowing smile. Then Abdul peered around his brother's body, peeking at Isa, smiling, his face graced with muddy lines, three stripes, on each cheek. He grinned goofily.

Isa rolled his eyes, not yet understanding what they were up to.

Eventually, Hamid turned around. He had created circles of mud on his brown cheeks. He winked at Isa, went back to work.

"You look stupid," Isa said. Was this what all their fuss was about?

"I do?" Hamid asked innocently.

"You're such an idiot," Isa replied, taking his eyes away, yanking on more weeds and throwing them aside.

Abdul gave up all pretence of working and walked over to Isa, grinning at him, the grin saying that there was something quite obvious that Isa was missing.

"What?" Isa asked exasperated.

Abdul merely giggled. Isa gave him a dirty look.

"We're just trying to be like you," Hamid said agreeably. "I mean, have you looked at yourself in the mirror lately or do you always go around with mud on your face? Or maybe it's some up-country thing we don't about."

Isa, feeling carefully at his face with his muddy fingers and realizing that they were making fun of him, felt embarrassed.

"I'll give you something to laugh about," Isa vowed. He sprang at Hamid, tackling the boy and forcing him down into the mud on his back. Straddling him, Isa got his hands muddy and went to work on the boy's face.

Abdul joined in, grabbing up handfuls of mud, and flinging them at Isa and Hamid.

Hamid cursed, tried to get Isa off his belly, but the curses were only playful, and soon they took to wrestling, flinging each other back and forth into the mud, laughing openly now at their foolishness. Somehow or another their shirts came off, and they were reduced to shorts, and all three winding up covered in mud from head to toe. At this point, Isa began to feel weak and faint from overdoing it. He laid in the mud and laughed but held up his hands, pleading with them to stop. Hamid would not, sitting on Isa's belly, pinning him to the ground, and grinning a savage, gleeful grin.

"Stop now," Isa said, breathless. "I don't feel quite right."

Hamid stopped, his expression changing from one of furious fun to serious concern. He got off Isa, but remained crouched by his side, hovering over him, looking at Isa's face.

"Are you all right?"

Isa nodded but did not say anything. Hamid put a hand on Isa's bare chest, then moved his hand up to the boy's face, as if he were perhaps checking for a temperature. It was a tender gesture, one of kindness, affection. He helped Isa to sit up, holding the boy in his arms, their bare flesh rubbing together.

"We better clean up before my mom sees us," Hamid said. He helped Isa get to his feet, told Abdul to grab their shirts.

There was an outdoor shower area, much like the one on Isa's grandparents' plantation, only this had an actual shower rather than large urns full of rainwater. The three boys stripped off their clothes, fought for their share of water, rinsed out their dirty clothes.

Isa tried hard not to look at Hamid's beautiful body but could not help himself. And the boy did not make it easy, with his constant rubbing up against him. Then it happened: Isa got an erection. He couldn't help it, couldn't stop it, couldn't hide it. He turned away from Hamid, pretending to be soaping up his privates while actually trying to hide them, but this only made him all the more horny.

"I'll help you," Hamid said. With soapy hands, he rubbed Isa's back and shoulders, all the way down to his buttocks. This only made it worse.

Then, a surprising thing: Hamid, standing just behind him, put his hands on Isa's hips, pulling him close, letting his own hardness push at Isa's backside.

"Stop it," Isa said, turning around, surprised and a bit angry.

Hamid, he saw, was hard as a rock. Abdul had finished already and had run into the house looking for clean clothes.

Hamid turned away, a guilty, embarrassed look on his face. Isa felt like he had reacted too harshly, but he had been surprised and suddenly afraid. He did not want anyone to put their thing in his backside again, not anymore.

The shower was enclosed, with an old shower curtain for a door, so they had some privacy. Not knowing why, Isa knelt down in front of the boy and took the hardness into his mouth, resisting Hamid's efforts to make him stop.

It took less than a minute for the boy to do his business. He turned his back immediately and began to wash himself off, as if trying to rid his body of some germ or disease. Isa stood up, uncomfortable. Had he gone too far?

"Don't ever tell anyone, or I'll kill you," Hamid said, leaving the shower and hurrying to get dressed.

ONE

THE MASTER ALWAYS called his wife "Mother." It was a term of endearment, a nod to the fact that she was the mother of his six sons. Looking through the kitchen window at the three boys playing in the mud, the Master said, "He seems to be coming along, Mother."

She snorted but did not reply.

"We shall have to think about school for him," he added.

"You're not really going to let him stay with us, are you?"

"And where is he to go?"

"Is that my concern?"

"Is it not?"

She snorted again and went back to making bread, kneading the large ball of dough she had on the table with angry jerks and slaps.

"You've been given so many blessings by Allah. Is it true that you're unwilling to share a few with this child?"

"He's not my child," she said forcefully.

The Master replied to this with a small, sad grin. It was a standard retort, a standard excuse not to care, not to get involved with the suffering of others, no matter how pitiable. If it was not blood, it did not matter. Charity began at home and stayed at home. One did not waste one's resources on the offspring of strangers, especially if those strangers were whores and G.I.s.

"He's bad blood, and make no mistake," she said, hefting the dough and slapping it down on the table with unnecessary force.

Bad blood. In other words, his parents had been unreliable, had left him an orphan. Their blood was bad. Their blood ran through the boy's veins. He would turn out bad, too, no matter what one did to help him. He had bad blood; that was the end of the matter, plain and simple.

"I thought we agreed that you would never utter such nonsense in my presence again," the Master reminded her, now irked with her, with her unkindness. He was not surprised by it, but on those occasions when it showed itself, he found it loathsome indeed.

"I've already taken care of six boys. Now there's the grandkids. Ahmed's got another on the way. Did you forget? Who has time for this riffraff trash? He's a heroin addict, said it himself! Don't you have any sense? How can you bring that sort of person into our house? Don't you know what sort of effect he'll have on the boys? Are you insane?"

She was taking that tone with him which meant that she was not about to back down. Rarely did she disobey. Rarely did she fight. When she did, it was because she believed herself to be in the right, and nothing her husband said would make any difference to her whatsoever. He could insist all he wanted, but she would not be swayed, not when her mind was made up.

"So what do you suggest?" he asked.

"Make him leave," she replied evenly, without so much as a pause for thought.

"And where will he go?"

"That's not our problem, is it?"

"I can't make him leave," he said quietly.

"Well, that's you," she said, just as quietly, a hint of malice—a touch of a threat—in her voice.

The Master frowned, then left the kitchen without reply. He went out onto the porch, found his "thinking chair," sat down upon it. It offered a nice view of the gardens and was shaded from the sun, and whenever he needed time for his own thoughts, he retreated to this space.

His wife was a good woman, but there was a hard streak in her that was like biting on tinfoil. Every now and again, he found himself recoiling from something she said or did, surprised at the depth of her hatefulness, but she was simply not him. She had swallowed down society's prejudices whole and entire, and did not question them. Like many others, she assumed that any half and half was the product of a foreign serviceman and a prostitute and deserved to be treated as such. She assumed that any Thai woman who married a *farang* was a prostitute. She assumed that "bad blood" ran in families, and that if the parents were bad, the children would be bad too. She assumed that Muslims were superior to Buddhists and were more righteous in the eyes of Allah. She assumed that most Thais were nothing more than decadent consumers who could care less about morality. She assumed that all her prejudices were valid and were not open to questioning.

She was a letter-of-the-law-er, as the Master thought of them: those who adhered rigidly to rules but did not understand the spirit behind them. It was all well and good for Allah to be compassionate and make exceptions to His rules, but the ordinary man in the street was duty bound to obey . . . or else. There were no extenuating circumstances, no second chances, no leniency; one obeyed. One did not question.

This sort of thinking had led to all sorts of foolishness over the centuries: Muslims and Christians killing each other, Jews and Muslims killing each other, Muslims and Hindus at each other's throats. It was the sort of foolishness that led young men and women, the Master thought with a feeling of shame, to blow themselves up in crowded marketplaces, hoping thereby to achieve Paradise, as if Allah would grant Paradise to someone whose last act in life had led to the death of innocent people.

They just did not understand! Man had been created out of love, and not for any other reason. Did the Creator need mere man to praise Him? Of course not! Did the Creator need mere man to keep Him company, to assuage His loneliness? The thought was ridiculous. What had led the Creator to make man and woman, if not a desire to share life and being with others? What, if not love? Love, the Master knew, was one of those rare things that only increased the more it was shared around. It was not like money, it was not like food. It was altogether different. The more one gave love away, the more it grew, the larger it became, the sweeter, the more tender, the more glorious and joyous and gratifying. Love alone had this quality. And for what other reason had Allah created humankind, if not because of Allah's great love, if not to break open His love like the breaking open of a coconut, to spill it freely and generously to one and all?

Rules were for the miscreants, the lowlifes who needed them, the unruly and the disobedient who needed a chain around their neck to keep them in line. But as soon one discovered the truth about love, rules became superfluous. It would not occur to the Master to do anything that would displease the Beloved; he did not need rules or commandments to keep him from hateful, evil actions. He did need the threat of the eternal fires of *Gehenna* to keep himself from murdering someone or committing adultery with another man's wife or cheating someone in a business deal. He would be too ashamed of himself to do such things, too ashamed to stand in the presence of Allah—Was there any place where Allah was not present?—too humiliated to give in to such low, base things.

He loved his wife and children, valued their good opinion of him. What would possess him to indulge in some unworthy passion and thus embarrass himself in their presence? And how much more so would he refrain from embarrassing himself in the eyes of Allah, the Supreme Beloved, the Creator, the Sustainer, the Lord of the Universe?

Since Allah had created each and every person, it was obvious that Allah loved that person; why bring that person into existence otherwise? Why give life to something that would displease Him? And if Allah loved all of them, surely the Master could do no less. What was so hard to understand about that? Why did his wife close her heart to love? What was lost when love was given away? Nothing. Could one ever be guilty of loving too much? But it was absurd. Yet there were those who were frugal with love, who held on to it with clenched fists, as if in giving it away they might lose it, as if there was only a finite amount of love, that it could be squandered.

Love wastefully—that was the Master's motto. Give love away. Let it pour out upon one and all. Where was the harm? The Master had discovered that love was a bottomless pit, that the more love he gave away, the more there was left to give.

This was how he often thought of the Beloved: a well of love. No matter how many came to slake their thirst, there was always room for one more. And in the beginning, when the Beloved was alone, that well of love was there. Now, having created so many beings, the well had become a vast meeting ground of joyful friends and grateful recipients. Now the Beloved would never be alone again. Time only increased the number of those who came to this well to assuage their thirst. And the more who came the more joyful everyone else became. The well was surrounded by a merry band of lovers who lived in the shadow of the Beloved and were content.

But so few understood this. So very few. Not even the Master's wife, his companion of decades, could bring herself to comprehend this, to believe it, to abandon herself to the claims that love had on her from every quarter. She loved her children, true enough, and her grandchildren, and her husband's relatives and her own. She loved freely and willingly, but she only loved her own. There was no room in her heart for those beyond her circle. There was no desire on her part to expand that circle. She did not see any need to do so.

According to the letter of the law, she was right: She had cared for her own, had been a good mother, had tended to the needs of her children and grandchildren, was above reproach in the matter. She would be rewarded accordingly. To have been faithful in caring for the matters entrusted to her was no small achievement, the Master knew. He had done the same, yet felt as though he had done only what was expected. So much more could have been done, could still be done. The love he felt for his wife and children brought him great joy. Why should that love stop at the front door to his own home? Why should it not go out and embrace the world and every living thing in it?

"Or am I just a fool?" he asked quietly, peering at his gardens, watching the boys trudge off to the shower to clean up.

TWO

"ISA, WHY DON'T you sit with me?"

The Master invited the boy to sit on the porch and relax. He could see that the boy was weak, still not fully recovered, had been overdoing it while rough-housing with Hamid and Abdul.

Isa sat on the wood of the porch, at the Master's feet, situating himself so that he could stare off to the side at the gardens. The smell of the nearby tomatoes came to him, and he drank it in. Creepers on the porch's trellis had their own smell, and this too Isa drank in.

The Master said nothing to the boy. They enjoyed the silence and the scenery together. Every now and again the Master let his eyes drift over to Isa. Such a beautiful boy, although much too thin and scraggly looking. When he filled out—when he began to eat properly for a boy his age and size—he would be a handsome addition to the family: strange, in his way, with his gray-green eyes and curly hair, and obviously an outsider, exotic, like some creature from the deep jungle or a traveler from across the sea.

"Tell me, Isa, what do you know of Allah?" the Master asked, after the silence had grown long.

"Nothing, sir," the boy replied.

"Call me Papa," the Master said.

The boy frowned. His lips looked like they wanted to do just that but could not. The boy said nothing.

"So, you know nothing, eh? Nothing about the Creator, the One who made you, who fashioned you in your mother's womb, who brought you forth and gave you life, and desires your love in return for all His gifts? You know nothing of this Being, this extraordinary Creator?"

Isa shook his head.

"Tell me, Isa, where did you come from?"

Isa thought about this for a moment, then said that he had come from his parents, that they had created him.

"And where did they come from?"

From Isa's grandparents, of course.

And where did Isa's grandparents come from?

Eventually, as they continued to go backward, Isa began to understand: At some point, there had to be the first man, the first woman, and where had that first man and first woman come from? Did they create themselves? Did they climb out of some primordial ooze somewhere? Wasn't it more likely that someone, or something, had created them, had brought them into existence?

"That someone was Allah," the Master said. "And that is why we honor Allah and submit ourselves to Allah. That is what it means to be a Muslim: to submit oneself to Allah. To revere the decrees of Allah. To reverence the word Allah has spoken in our midst: the Koran. It is the Koran that requires us to pray five times a day, and now that you are feeling better, I shall ask you to join us. Would you like that?"

Isa nodded. To be included made him feel important.

"Well, someday perhaps we shall make a good Muslim boy out of you, eh?"

Isa smiled. He wanted that, too. He didn't care what Muslims believed or what he had to do; he just wanted to belong. Like most kids, that's all he really wanted: to belong, to have a place where he fit in, to have a set of surroundings that he was familiar with, that he could identify himself by, that gave a sense of continuity to his life.

THREE

THE FOLLOWING DAY was Sunday, and Isa was roused early, with the other boys, who put on their *kurtas* in the darkness of the early morning, preparing to go to the mosque with their father. Isa loved wearing his *kurta*, though it was not "his," belonging as it did to Hamid. He could not wait to have one of his own. When he put it on he felt like a new person, a different person. When he stood in front of the mirror and saw the white of the fabric bringing out the brown of his skin, he could almost believe that he had embarked on a new life, that his luck had changed, his bad karma had been expunged.

They did little more than brush their teeth before heading out the door to walk the three blocks to the mosque in darkness, ignored by the dogs, smiled at by vendors getting an early start.

At the mosque, more than thirty boys and men were already waiting for the Imam to arrive and lead the prayers. Isa again sat next to Muhammad as they did their ablutions in silence, Isa watching Muhammad's gestures carefully, trying to get them exactly right and not make a fool of himself. No one seemed to pay him any attention. There were no questions in their eyes, not the sort that he had grown used to while out on the street. There were no silent invitations for sex, no come-ons, no hesitant interest, no shy glances filled with yearning. Here, he was just another boy among many other boys. The Master was just another man among many other men. They were here to offer their early morning prayers, not to socialize. Isa could see that most were known to each other, that nods of greeting were all that was necessary. They were a big family, in a way, had been through this ritual day after day, year after year.

Isa followed Muhammad as the prayers were said. He was never quite sure of when to stand, when to bend over, when to kneel down, when to prostrate, but by watching Muhammad carefully out of the corner of his eye, he could pretend that he knew what he was doing, that he belonged here among these people, that he was not an outsider.

After the morning prayers, the gathering quickly broke up. The Kloy boys offered more casual greetings to their friends, but it was Sunday, and each was in a hurry to go home and tend to Sunday affairs: dinners, get-togethers, parties, shopping, movies.

The light was faint in the sky when Isa followed the Kloy brothers home. Mrs. Kloy had breakfast waiting on the table, and they immediately sat down to it. The Master led them in a brief prayer. Muhammad noted that he had been invited to the wedding of a friend that was to be held later that day. He wondered what he should wear and how much money he should give as a gift. Bilal said he had tests to study for and had to get back to the dorm. Abdul, whenever his mother and father weren't looking, tossed grains of rice at Hamid, trying to provoke him. Mrs. Kloy oversaw the gathering like a waitress at an especially hospitable restaurant.

Thus the day went on, typical, normal family life, but for Isa, it was wondrous. It was heavenly. It was comforting in its routineness: safe, pleasant, soothing. No one shouted, no one hit, possessions did not go flying. No words of ridicule were sent his way. He was not called half and half, bird-shit foreigner, cocksucker. Aside from his quietness and his unusual physical appearance, he was just like the others.

Abdul ran off to watch cartoons. Muhammad and Bilal remained at the table, talking to their father about their studies, their friends, the activities of the Islamic youth group they both participated in and were members of.

Hamid got to his feet, told Isa to follow him, so Isa did. They went out onto the porch, wandered into the gardens and out into the back of the property where there was a pond and several banana and mango trees . . . and privacy. They did not speak as they sat down, side by side, near the pond, gazing over its still waters. Isa had the sense that there were many things Hamid wanted to say but could not or was not yet ready. He himself wanted to say something, but what? He did not know.

To be alone with the other boy was somehow frightening but also exciting, unnerving. It made his heart beat a little bit faster. It made him breathless with anticipation, weak with fear. He wanted Hamid to like him or at least to not hate him. Yet he wanted so much more than that. He wanted Hamid to take off his clothes. He wanted sex, pleasure, the release of orgasm, the delight of warm lips on his penis or the feel of the boy's hard flesh poking at his backside. Why did he want these things? He did not know. But if Hamid was pleased by them, and if it helped Hamid to accept him and to find value in friendship with him, then Isa was willing.

Isa didn't really know how to be friends with anyone, had

never been taught that it wasn't necessary to offer sex as an incentive. All the way back to Som and his pals, Isa had been offering sex for approval, sex for friendship, sex for affection. He did not know how to relate to another person in any other way. It seemed, in his mind, only natural, only normal, that boys would demand sex as the price of their friendship and affection. Even if he found this humiliating and hurtful, he dared not complain. Even if he preferred not to bend over and let a boy have his way, he would quietly submit and endure because friendship was precious to him, and he would do anything to obtain it, anything at all.

Hamid was giving off sexual vibes, so Isa put a hand on the boy's bare leg just below the fabric of his shorts. The leg was soft, but strong, warm, pleasant to touch. Isa looked down into Hamid's lap, saw the flesh harden there. He glanced at the boy, but Hamid would not look at him. He knew Hamid wanted sex, was desperate for it, but was afraid to ask, so he let his hand climb up the leg to grasp the erection beneath the fabric, squeezing it gently, exploringly, glancing up again at the boy, his eyes full of questions.

Hamid closed his eyes, held his breath, trembled.

"Do you want me to . . . "

"Yes," Hamid said quietly, urgently. "Please."

The "please" was offered as if he were terrified of offending Isa, of not getting this bit of pleasure that his body so desperately wanted.

"Can anyone see us?" Isa asked.

Hamid, still with his eyes closed, shook his head.

Isa did what the boy wanted, and when it was over, Hamid

pushed him away, then laid back on the grass, panting. Isa watched him, watched the rise and fall of his belly as he breathed. He could see part of it because Hamid's shirt was lifted up. He watched the way the fabric of Hamid's shorts fell down to reveal most of his legs as he lay there, on his back, knees drawn up, legs askew.

"I'm not a homo or anything," Hamid said after awhile. "I just like to be sucked, that's all."

Isa said nothing.

"I made Abdul do it once, but he told on me, and my dad got real mad about it. He's always telling on me for everything, the little shit."

"Why did your dad get mad?" Isa asked.

"He said it was why the people of Sodom were destroyed by Allah: for being homos and cocksuckers."

Isa frowned. "Who are the people of Sodom?"

"Haven't you ever read the Koran?"

Isa shook his head.

"They were some people, a long time ago. Allah destroyed their city because they were fags. My dad said Allah would destroy me too if I did things like that."

"Things like what?"

"Like what the people of Sodom did."

"And what did they do?"

"Well, they were fags, you know, fucking each other and all that. Allah hates fags, hates homosexuals, cross-dressers, fucking fairies. Those kind of people will never get to Paradise, they'll just burn in *Gehenna* because they're evil people."

This was delivered with such conviction that Isa shuddered.

Would Allah condemn him to eternal torment since he was a fag? Would Allah punish him for all the things he'd done: the men, their money, the blow jobs, the sex?

He lowered his eyes, stared at his own lap, feeling suddenly ashamed of himself. That feeling was only too familiar. It came upon him so easily. What he was, deep down inside, was something shameful and disgusting: a fag. A homo. A queer. A pervert. A cocksucker. A butt boy. His mother had been a whore, so what else was to be expected of her offspring? He was only fifteen, but he'd already had sex with so many people, he had lost track of them all. There were Som and his friends. Chok and the other men. Gong. The men who picked him up. The other boys. Now Hamid, too. Had the number reached a hundred? Two hundred? Five hundred? How many blow jobs had he given, kneeling in alleys or behind cars or inside cars or in small apartments or in public bathrooms? How many men had raided his back door and buried their hardness there?

"You're not going to tell on me, are you?" Hamid asked, opening his eyes now and glancing over at Isa.

"Of course not," Isa said.

Hamid seemed satisfied with this answer, closed his eyes, said nothing further about it.

FOUR

THAT NIGHT, SINCE Bilal and Muhammad had gone back to their dorms, only Hamid and Abdul were left in the boys' room, and Isa put his mat down next to Hamid's, leaving Abdul on the far side.

Having spent most of the evening studying, the Kloy boys were sleepy. It did not take long for Abdul to fall asleep. Hamid settled down too and seemed to be sleeping. Only Isa stared up at the ceiling, his mind filled with restless thoughts, yearnings, desires, questions. Where was Gong now? Where were the others? How much longer could he stay with the Master and his family? Why did Mrs. Kloy give him such hateful, disapproving looks? Why was the Master so kind? Was there really a god named Allah who would punish him in the burning fires of *Gehenna* for ever and ever and ever? He tried to comprehend how long that could be: forever. Eternity. No matter how many years went by, it would only just be starting. Endless torment and pain, century after century, and it was only a tiny drop in the bucket. Forever and ever and ever. Would he be punished that way for being a homo, a queer, a boy who liked other boys? Would this Allah destroy him the way He had destroyed the people of Sodom? It frightened him to think about it. So he tossed and turned, restless with these questions, filled with his own needs and urges, his penis hard, wanting relief from its burden.

Many minutes went by before Hamid reached a hesitant hand over to Isa, laying it on Isa's hip, urging Isa to lie down on his back. Isa, mystified, did just that. Hamid, soundless, sat up and gazed down at him. He lifted Isa's shirt up, exposing his stomach. He urged Isa to let his shorts be pulled down, to let the hard flesh there be exposed. He urged Isa to remove his clothes entirely, and Isa did. Hamid did the same. Then, very quietly, so as not to rouse Abdul, Hamid put his head down on Isa's lap, inexpertly taking the flesh into his mouth, wanting to suck it. Isa whispered for him not to bite it, to be careful with his teeth. Hamid complied, but when Isa began to come, Hamid choked on it and pulled back, then cast a terrified glance at his sleeping brother. Abdul slept on, oblivious.

Isa took his business in hand to finish the job, letting the semen spill on his belly. Hamid, oddly enough, bent forward and began to lick at it. Isa allowed him to. When he had been cleaned up in this fashion, Hamid moved closer so that they could see each other, could embrace, could press their naked bodies together. His eyes, in the darkness, seemed filled with pain and confusion as well as delight and release. His hands were urgent, exploring Isa's body, feeling every muscle, every limb, every crevice. After many minutes of this, he said very quietly, "Let me fuck you."

Isa agreed, turning over, not making a sound, letting his body fit into the groove of Hamid's, letting the boy's hardness force its way inside. It hurt, but Isa did not care. Hamid, once he was inside, paused to cover them with his own blanket so that they could not be seen should Abdul wake up or their parents come into the room. He took his time, thrusting his hips back and forth against Isa, squeezing Isa around the chest, around the waist, occasionally letting his hands grab handfuls of flesh, as if in agony. Soon enough he began to breathe heavily into Isa's ear, clinging to him, trembling, driving himself deeper and deeper until at last he stopped, his whole body shuddering and trembling, hot, sweaty, the beating of his heart almost like a physical sound.

Hamid remained where he was, his body locked with Isa's, their flesh joined. It was as though he didn't want to let Isa go, but then he did, quickly pushing Isa away, back to his own mat, hurriedly putting on his shorts and shirt, turning his back to Isa as he settled down again on his own mat.

Isa slowly got dressed, feeling a bit hurt by this sudden coldness. He watched Hamid in the darkness, the light of the moon faint as it came through the open shutters. After a minute, he realized that Hamid was crying softly to himself.

"What's wrong?" Isa asked, confused. Had Isa somehow hurt him?

Hamid wouldn't answer.

"Did I hurt you?" Isa whispered, bending close to the boy, full of concern now.

Hamid shook his head but would not answer, would not look up at him.

"Then what?" Isa asked, irritated.

But Hamid would not say.

ONE

HAMID AHMAD KNEW that there was a word for what he was, but he didn't like that word, did not want to admit to himself that the word described him perfectly. *Homosexual.* It was hateful, dirty word, a swear word. If you really wanted to insult someone, just hurl that word. To actually be a homosexual, well, what could be more humiliating? More shameful? More embarrassing?

The word *tood* was a shortcut. It referred to one's ass, of course, but also to men who like being buggered, who liked getting it up the ass. It was also short for *gatoey*, a cross-dresser, a man who acted like a woman, a screaming queen. *Tood* was the word of choice; gay was far too Western, too confusing, its meaning too obscure. A homosexual, as far as Hamid was concerned, was a faggot, a boy who liked to wear dresses, a silly little sissy who liked giving blow jobs. There were, as yet, no other words in his vocabulary to describe the matter and he had yet to hear of men who were attracted to men and who preferred it that way and who did not see themselves as screaming queens and who did not like to dress up or wear wigs. The very idea of such a person had yet to cross his young mind. Based on what he knew, a homosexual was a *tood*, a silly thing, a ridiculous thing, a laughable, idiotic thing, in much the same way as most people's asses were laughable and idiotic things not to be taken too seriously.

He was a *tood*, a *gatoey*. He would soon be into his mother's lipsticks or trying on her dresses. That he took pleasure from having another boy give him a blow job was only confirmation of how despicable and disgraceful it all was, real boys got blow jobs from their girlfriends and bragged about them. Real boys got girls to hike up their skirts and be still long enough so that they could bang them and live to brag about it afterward. Real boys couldn't get enough of tits, boobs, hoochies, coconuts. They loved to "fly the kite" (masturbate) while looking at pictures in women's magazines of half-naked models with their heaving bosoms and thongs. They did not fly their kites while thinking about what it would be like to suck someone's penis.

All of this business frightened Hamid, and he wanted no part of it. Sure, he had crushes on boys his age, liked to lay in bed at night fantasizing about them and their bodies, but that didn't mean he was a *tood*. Someday he would be interested in girls too, like everyone else, only not now. Not today.

Of course it was a bit strange, this attraction to boys his own age, this attraction to their chests and bellies, this habit he'd developed of thinking about what it would be like to touch their buttocks or put his fist over their penises. Strange but probably normal, a phase that would pass, nothing to be worried about. He had no doubt that other boys were going through it but would never admit it. He had no doubt that Isa was going through it, harbored the same secret, terrible desires. If they could help each other through this period in their lives, what harm was there in that? Perhaps with a little bit of exploration, he would find himself turned off by boys and would move on to girls.

Part of his mind knew this was bullshit. Another part of his mind insisted that it had to be true, because if it were... well, it had to be true. That's all there was to it. It had to be. Hamid was not a *tood*, not a fag. Could not be. Could not bring disgrace upon himself and his family by being such a cursed, perverted thing.

If he was...

Well, he wasn't, so what was there to think about?

TWO

ON THE FOLLOWING morning, Hamid woke before the others. All night he had been restless, full of conflicting feelings. Buggering Isa had been wondrous, the pleasure of it so intense, so overwhelming that he couldn't stop thinking about it, reliving it, wanting to do it again. Yet the pleasure of it made him suspicious. Surely it was wrong. Surely it was sinful to indulge such a lust. Sodomy, after all, made the throne of Allah tremble, or so it was often said. For a man to bugger another man was so completely unnatural that it was hateful in the sight of God; there were few things that a man could do that would be more degrading, more shameful.

In the darkness, he looked over to where Isa lay. He wanted to make love again, wanted to force himself on the youth, wanted to feel that incredible pleasure, yet he didn't dare; their father would be waking them soon to get ready for morning prayers at the mosque, for breakfast, for school. Instead, he remembered what it had been like to take the boy's penis into his mouth, and he masturbated by himself, powerful feelings of lust sweeping through him, a lust so intense he could not deny its demands.

THREE

"HE CAN WEAR one of Hamid's *kurtas*," the Master said.

They were now eating breakfast, getting ready for school. It had been decided that Isa should go to school with Hamid, should sit beside him, try to follow along as best he could. Since they went to an Islamic school, there weren't many students anyway, and there was no need for him to register, not just yet.

Mrs. Kloy made a face but departed the kitchen to search for a *kurta* that Isa could wear.

"I won't get it dirty," Isa said, thinking the woman was

annoyed at having more dirty clothes to tend to.

"Don't you worry about that," the Master said kindly.

"I didn't mean to make her mad."

"She's not mad."

Isa glanced across the table, saw Abdul roll his eyes, which told him that she was indeed mad and that the Master was just trying to be polite.

Isa was beginning to understand that Mrs. Kloy didn't like him, not at all. She would not look at him directly, rarely spoke to him, and tolerated his presence but nothing more. Because of this, Isa found that he did not really like her either, that he was afraid of her, did not want to be left alone in a room with her, found all sorts of reasons not to talk to her, not to impose himself, to be as invisible as possible around her.

Mrs. Kloy returned with a *kurta*, handing it to Hamid without comment, as if she didn't want to give it directly to Isa. They finished breakfast and got dressed. Hamid and Abdul received kisses from their mother on their way out the door. Isa received a turning away of her head as she hurried back to the kitchen, as if something might be burning on the stove or as if there were some important duty that could not be kept waiting.

The Master gave each of them ten baht as lunch money. Isa pocketed his coin happily. The Master offered him a smile as he saw them out the door, a wave as he remained on the porch while the boys trudged off down the lane, through the gates, out into the city beyond.

FOUR

ISLAMIC SCHOOL WAS not quite what Isa expected. It had been a long time since he'd gone to school, and it was quickly obvious that he was way behind his peers. The first class was Arabic. Hamid was up to level six already. Isa couldn't distinguish one letter of the Arabic alphabet from the next, much less read or understand anything of it. This produced much laughter among the students until the teacher told them to quiet down and not be so rude, that Isa would have to start at the beginning, that Hamid and Abdul would have to tutor him and help him to catch up.

One of the most unexpected things about school was the teacher, a man in his forties with a beard and a piercing set of eyes: Khun Jummah. Isa remembered that beard and those eyes, remembered how they had spotted him outside Lumphini Park. He had gone home with this man two or three times. Had laid in the man's bed while the man pawed at his body and all but raped him in his haste to get his rocks off. Of course. It must have been this man who had picked up Isa that evening, who had kicked him out into the street. The mosque was close by; Isa had wandered there in a drug-induced fog. Of course.

The man showed no sign of recognition. Neither did Isa. The man seemed, from time to time, a bit nervous. So was Isa. The man avoided making eye contact. So did Isa.

Was he mistaken? He did not think so. Even the sound of the man's voice was familiar, a husky sort of growl, impatient to be obeyed, listened to, respected.

Isa sat next to Hamid the whole day, was surprised at how well-behaved the Muslim students were. They all wore *kurtas* and prayer hats. They stopped at noon for lunch, followed by noon prayers, which were led by the teacher. They did not have recess or recreation, not until school was finished. Then they could play soccer, if they liked, although they had to say afternoon prayers beforehand.

Boys were in one class, girls in another. The boys were taught by a man, the girls by a woman. The boys wore *kurtas*; the girls wore veils and long dresses, and some wore complete *hijab*. They did not interact. They did not so much as look at each other. They were kept in separate rooms, ate at separate times, did not pray together. When Isa craned his neck to watch the girls leaving their classroom to go to lunch, Hamid told him not to stare, not to look, lest he get into trouble.

At the end of the day, the students dispersed, but the Kloy brothers and Isa were asked by the teacher to remain behind.

"Actually, you and your brother may leave," the teacher said to Hamid, nodding his head at the door, as if he meant for them to leave straight away. "I just need to talk to our new student for a few minutes. You can wait for him outside."

Hamid and Abdul left, and Isa was alone with this man, Khun Jummah.

"What are you doing at my school?" Jummah asked abruptly, now giving Isa his full attention. There was no one else about, no one to overhear anything they might say.

"I've been staying with the Imam and his family."

"So you're not from around here?"

Isa shook his head.

"You remember me?"

Isa nodded.

"Would you like to go to this school?"

Again, Isa nodded.

"Then keep your mouth shut."

Wordless, Isa agreed.

Silence.

"You are far behind the others," the teacher said.

"I'm sorry. I know."

"You may have to stay late on some evenings. I can tutor you. Otherwise you can't possibly hope to be put in the right grade. I'll have to send you back a couple of years."

"I can catch up," Isa replied. It would be humiliating to be sent back.

"If you work hard, I suppose you could."

"I will," Isa said.

"We'll see," Jummah replied. "Before you go, let me warn you, Isa. You're not a Muslim. You don't belong here in this school. If Mr. and Mrs. Kloy find out about you—about what you used to do—they will demand that you leave. Do you understand me?"

Isa nodded.

"If I were you, I would keep my mouth shut. I wouldn't be telling the Imam or anyone else what you used to do. If word went around the community about it, you would not be welcome here any more."

Isa stared at the floor between them, embarrassed.

"Are you related to the Kloys?"

Isa shook his head.

"They just took you in?"

"Yes."

"Did they even know you?"

Isa shook his head again.

"Well, you'll find that our Imam is a very good-hearted man. Don't embarrass him by telling tales of what you used to do, okay? Don't shame him by talking about yourself. If he ever found out about it, he would have to make you leave. Have you told him anything?"

"Of course not," Isa said right away.

"Good. Don't. That's my advice. And you're not to tell anyone about our little secret. Is that understood?"

Slowly Isa nodded.

"If you were to tell someone, first of all I don't think they'd believe you. Second, I would reveal your background, and then no one would believe you at all. I would tell them that you used to be a whore and a drug addict too, if I remember correctly. The last time I saw you, you could hardly put your clothes on. Third, if you were to make me lose face that way, well, who knows what I might do about it? A man's reputation is all he has. If you destroy a man's reputation, you'd best be prepared to pay the price for it. Do you understand me?"

Isa again nodded, his belly full of fear.

The man now took hold of Isa's arm and began to squeeze it. He kept squeezing until it became painful, but Isa didn't dare pull away. Jummah was now so close to him, he could see the dew of perspiration in his beard, how some of the hairs were already gray.

"In this community," Jummah said, "there are things we dare not speak of, much less do. But those of us who do them must guard our secrets carefully. I'm not sure I could impress upon you the consequences of failing in that matter."

"It hurts," Isa whispered.

"Do you think so?" the man replied. He squeezed harder, twisting Isa's arm at an uncomfortable angle. "I should expose you right now; the Imam would have no choice but to make you leave. If I had any sense, that's what I'd do. But I'm not going to do that. I'm going to trust you to keep your mouth shut. Can I trust you to do that?"

He twisted Isa's arm a bit farther. Isa nodded, grimacing at the pain swirling up his arm and into his shoulder. Then the man relented and gave Isa a long, considered look.

"Don't you forget what I said," he said at last.

"I won't," Isa replied very quietly.

"You can leave now."

FIVE

"WHAT DID HE want?" Hamid asked when Isa rejoined them and they began to walk home. The route was already familiar, for the school was right next to the mosque.

"Nothing," Isa said, saying the word in a way that suggested it wasn't worth discussing because it was so trivial.

"What?" Hamid pressed.

Isa shrugged. "Told me I had to study hard or I would be sent back a couple of years to make up the work. That kind of stuff."

"You *will* have to study hard," Hamid replied. "You're way behind."

"Even I know more Arabic than he does," Abdul added.

"Yeah, but you'll always be stupid," Hamid said, "no matter how much Arabic you know."

"Will not."

"Will to."

"Will not."

"Will to."

"Says who?"

"Says me."

Abdul marched on ahead, knowing he wasn't going to get the better of any argument with his brother.

Isa watched him, amused, wishing he had a little brother he could torment but also wishing he was someone's little brother and would be tormented in such a fashion. What he wouldn't give to belong, to have a family. To have blood—the thickest thing, the only real thing. Only your blood could love you truly. Only your blood would put up with you. Only your blood would never abandon you. Yet, his had.

"You can use my old books," Hamid said, breaking into his thoughts. "You'll have to start with the alphabet. It's not that hard."

Isa said nothing.

"*Alif, bah, tah* . . . it's a lot shorter than the Thai alphabet. Just takes a little practice."

"You'll teach me?"

"Of course."

SIX

AT HOME, MRS. Kloy told them to say prayers and get changed. She did not pray with them.

Before removing their *kurtas*, Hamid led them in the late afternoon prayers. Hamid and Abdul had their own prayer rugs, which they kept stowed away in the bedroom. They provided a third for Isa, made an orderly row, and said the prayers, Isa following along as best he could, with Hamid rushing the prayers, speaking the Arabic words so quickly it was hard to distinguish one from the next. Isa could see that this was a ritual they went through to please their parents, not because they enjoyed it or cared about it one way or the other.

After the prayers, they removed their *kurtas*, piling them in the dirty-clothes basket for Mrs. Kloy to tend to. When he saw Hamid's bare belly and chest, Isa got a hard-on and turned away, hoping no one would see it. Abdul paraded around the room naked, having not yet learned to be ashamed of his body, though puberty would soon change that, before marching off to the bathroom, a towel over his shoulder.

Alone with Hamid, Isa tried to find a pair of shorts that he could claim, but Hamid came up behind him, putting his arms around Isa's waist, pressing his bare body close, poking at Isa with his hard business.

"Someone will see," Isa whispered, embarrassed.

"Not if we hurry," Hamid replied, urging Isa to kneel down so that he could relieve the lust swelling inside his body.

Embarrassed, Isa knelt down, hurrying to do what the

boy wanted. Hamid had a towel around his hips, which he held open. He stood with his back to the door, so that if anyone came in, they would not be able to see what was happening.

It took only a minute or two, then they changed positions, not because Isa wanted to, but because Hamid wanted to. Isa was worried that Mrs. Kloy would come into the room. Hamid was oblivious, on fire with his youthful lust, determined to have his way, uncaring of the consequences. Afterward, they looked at each other sheepishly. Once the passion was spent, they were quickly embarrassed, shy again, uncertain.

They showered and sat down with their school books. At six, Mrs. Kloy served dinner. Afterward they were allowed to watch TV or play cards. Hamid took Isa to the bedroom and spread out their sleeping mats, making him sit so that they could study Arabic. They started with the first letter, *Alif*. A as in *Allah*. They removed their shirts, because it was hot. They carried on as two brothers would or, more precisely, the way two people did once they had engaged in sex. After such an intimate encounter, how could there be borders? What need for shyness or uncertainty? They were like old friends who had known each other for a million years. How could they not be after sucking each other's penises? They were no longer shy about staring at each other, touching each other, asking embarrassing questions. They had a sort of claim on each other now. The relationship was different. They acted more like young lovers than two friends. So they studied.

When Abdul came along, wanting to play, wanting attention, wanting to be included, they happily excluded him.

Tormented him. Insulted him. Purposefully tried to make him angry, to hurt his feelings.

"I thought you didn't like this *kaffir* piece of trash," Abdul said to Hamid, getting frustrated.

"Don't call him that!"

"Oh, he's your boyfriend now?"

"You shut up!"

"Everyone knows you're a *tood*!"

"I'll shut you up if you don't stop it."

"*Tood*!" Abdul could sense that he had struck a nerve. Of course, calling anyone a *tood* was guaranteed to provoke a reaction.

"I'm going to jam your head up your own *tood* if you don't shut up," Hamid spat.

"I'd like to see you try!"

"Fucking wanker."

"I'm gonna tell Ma you were swearing."

"Go ahead, you wanker. Why don't you go fly your kite?"

"I'm gonna tell."

"Fine."

"*Tood*!"

"Wanker."

And on it went.

Seeing that his tactics were not achieving the desired result, Abdul grabbed up the Arabic book they had been studying from.

"Give it back, you wanker," Hamid said, annoyed.

"Stop calling me a wanker!"

"Stop calling me a *tood*."

"I can teach him too, you know."

"Why don't you?" Hamid countered.

Abdul, sensing that he had found an opening, now sat down with them, putting the book back where it was. He proceeded to proudly show off his Arabic skills, every now and again ridiculing Isa for being so stupid.

When it was time for bed, Isa had had quite enough of the *Alif, Bah, Tah* business. They had one more set of prayers to recite; there were five sets, spread throughout the day. They did their ablutions in the bathroom, said their prayers, and went to bed.

In the darkness, with their mats right next to each other, Hamid let one hand stray over to Isa, landing it on Isa's belly and leaving it there, every so often rubbing his fingers against Isa's skin.

Isa fell asleep.

SEVEN

"COME ON," HAMID said.

Isa followed.

After a week of school, it was Friday morning; no school today. They had just returned from the early morning prayers at the mosque. Abdul, as was his habit, had raced to the television to see the cartoons.

Hamid, dressed now in nothing but shorts that showed his youthful body to good effect, marched through the gardens, through the rows of tomatoes, through his mother's patch of chilies, past the apple trees, out into the back, to the pond. On the way, he had grabbed a dried-out banana leaf. When Isa asked what it was for, Hamid merely shrugged and smiled.

Instead of sitting in their usual spot by the pond, Hamid led Isa around to the other side, where a large mango tree held forth. Isa had discovered that it was Mrs. Kloy's favorite, that it produced more mangoes than anyone knew what to do with. Hamid darted up into its branches, something his mother would never do. He retrieved a plastic bag that he kept stashed in one of the high branches and jumped back to the ground, smiling. It contained a small bag of tobacco, a paper cutter, and cigarette lighter.

Isa frowned uncertainly.

Hamid smiled. "If you tell anyone, I'll kill you."

"You're going to smoke?"

Hamid smiled broadly. He sat down at the base of the tree where there was a board propped against it. Hamid took the board, then fiddled with the dried banana leaf, cutting a small rectangle from it. Next he put a pinch of tobacco in it, smoothed it out, then rolled the banana leaf up into a cigarette. After a few tries, he got one end lit. He inhaled deeply, smiled and then offered the makeshift cigarette to Isa, who accepted. It had been a long time since he had last smoked, but he liked the taste of it and was pleased to puff at the banana- leaf cigarette, smiling dopily as he did so.

Then they finished that one; Hamid made another.

"Won't anyone see us?" Isa asked.

"Nah," Hamid said, shrugging. "Nobody pays attention."

The banana leaf burned slowly, and the second cigarette

lasted a good ten minutes. They sat side by side, smoking it, glancing at each other's bodies, both of them barechested, both of them wearing shorts—Hamid's shorts—both of them growing more comfortable with each other, feeling some strange, inexplicable happiness in the presence of the other. It did not occur to them that they were falling in love. They would have laughed had such a thing been mentioned, would have denied it. They were blind to what they were about, but that didn't diminish the truth of it, the reality of it, the pleasing, sweet sensations it produced.

They were both fifteen, beyond puberty. They were now sexual beings. They were searching for the other, for completeness, seeking to unite their bodies into a harmonious whole. That was the way of life: All creatures were driven to finding this completeness in the other. It was the looking into the eyes of another, finding approval there, acceptance, validation. I'm okay; you're okay. We're okay. The world's okay. You're the same as me. I'm the same as you. We're not freaks, aberrations, mistakes. We're just different. If I'm weird, then so are you. But if that's okay—if I don't mind your being weird—then it's okay for me to be weird too.

All these things were going on, without their knowing it, without their consent or approval or awareness. They were bonding, imprinting, fixing the other in their mind, memorizing the face of the other, the chest, the penis, the legs, the feet, the muscles, the color, the smell, the hair, the sound of the voice, the light in the eyes, the habits and mannerisms, the likes and dislikes, the hopes, fears, and truths that each carried. It was a delightful process. Each new piece of information was stored away, as if it were a precious jewel of untold value.

Into this symbiotic relationship, there was not yet room for a third. That would come, in time, but not now. Now it was the sweetness of being with the beloved, the delight of his caresses, the tenderness of his love, the sweetness of his being, the joy of his sex.

"Why did your mom name you Isa?" Hamid asked, giving Isa an earnest look.

Isa shrugged.

"She must have had a reason," Hamid pressed.

Isa didn't want to talk about his mom, most especially did not want to explain that his name was a stupid little joke. "Your mom is going to smell us, you know."

"No, she's not."

"Oh please."

"She's not, because we're going to go swimming."

"In the pond?"

"Where else?"

"Aren't there snakes in there or something?"

"Could be," Hamid said mischievously.

"No way, not me," Isa vowed.

"Yes way," Hamid replied. He stood, hooked his thumbs in his shorts, removed them, and stood there in his underwear. "Come on."

"I'm not going swimming!"

"Come on. For me. There's nothing in there. You have to, anyway, because my mom will smell you; she can smell smoke from a mile away."

With more prodding, Isa let himself be convinced and eventually waded into the pond after Hamid. They spent almost an hour playing together, trying to dunk each other, rejoicing in the feeling of their bodies rubbing and pressing together, laughing, completely forgetting themselves now, lost in the joy and delight of the other. Two souls had merged to become one. Two entities had found harmonious coexistence. Yin and yang. Sixty-nine.

What was all this, if not preparation for following the Beloved, for losing oneself in the Beloved, for spinning around the Beloved like a whirling dervish, seeking to annihilate oneself, to merge, to let go of ego, boundaries, borders, to be completely porous so as to experience the completely overwhelming experience of being really and truly loved? And who could love really and truly, if not the Beloved? All other loves paled in comparison. All other loves were games, practice, the first tentative footsteps on a path that led to much grander things.

EIGHT

THE MASTER, WHO was taking his morning walk in his gardens, heard the boys playing in the pond and let his footsteps take him in that direction. He did not disturb them, did not impose on them. Rather, he stayed away, content to watch them.

Isa looked so happy. So did Hamid. They had taken to each other, like brothers. That had always been Hamid's problem: there was such an age difference between him and the others. His two oldest were a year apart. Muhammad and Bilal were also a year apart. Then came Hamid, three years later, then Abdul, four years after that. Hamid had always been too young for Muhammad and Bilal, too old for Abdul. Now he had a friend of his own, someone his own age. It was a delight to watch them as they carried on. It made the Master feel as though there was good in the world. It made the Master grateful that Allah had sent this child their way.

Were they out of the woods? Oh no. Not by any means. But they had made a start. With love, with time, with attention, perhaps Isa's wounds would heal. Perhaps Isa would become a Muslim, a real Muslim, one who submits to Allah, one who acknowledges that there is no god but Allah, that Muhammad was His messenger. Perhaps Isa would settle down, become part of their family, would let them love him, would let them include him, would let their love heal the hurts in his heart.

What could they do, but try? Of course, Allah had His own plans for Isa, and those plans might be a far cry from the Master's. Those plans might take Isa away from them. The Master did not concern himself with that now. For now, it was enough to see the boy laughing, going to school, going to prayers; enough to see his belly filling out, his muscles growing stronger; enough to see some hope returning to his eyes, some sense of self-esteem and self-respect, some sense that the world could be a good place, that one didn't need heroin to get by, that one could be happy without the enticements of the flesh and the belly and the world.

So, the Master watched and smiled. Allah was to be praised,

so praise Him the Master did. The Beloved knew what He was doing. The Beloved wanted only good things for His children, only sweet things, joyful things, a life of honest work and honest rewards. The Beloved could transform a creature like Isa into whatever He chose, for the Beloved was free to do as He pleased. There was no questioning the ways of Love, its currents, its movements, its healing powers, it ability to crush, revive, hurt, heal. Allah could give life, could take it away. Allah could revive a dead soul, could make a living one turn to stone. Allah was glorious, not to be questioned, not to be doubted.

Praise be to Allah! Al-hamdu li-lah!

ONE

IT WAS THE eggs, Nida Tongwanich decided on the plane back to Bangkok. The fucking eggs. The eggs that had to be "soft boiled" precisely two minutes, "soft peeled," served with a "tad" of salt next to a slice of white bread "toasted on one side." She'd take a "tad" of salt and shove it straight up his ass. Not just salt. The fucking eggs and piece of bread, too, and his fucking house, and his fucking dotty mother, and the old bitty across the street who was constantly spying on them with her fucking binoculars. Not to mention the constant shivering and shaking from the fucking cold, the constant hunger from the bland food, and the constant isolation of being a foreign woman living among Danes who were always looking down their flawless white noses at her.

Nida would do just about anything for money, but the sheer boredom of being Martin Hurgett's wife had proved too much, Denmark or no, rich or not. She'd gladly go back to whoring just to get away from him and the extra fifteen pounds he could never lose and the frigging smell of his pipe, which she could no longer stand, and everything else that had been driving her mad for the past four years, like the ridiculous moustache that annoyed her every time he wanted to kiss her, which seemed like every other minute, and his insistence that his underwear be ironed.

Only on the plane did she settle down. She was seated in economy class—of course, Martin was so cheap he wouldn't spring for anything better. He'd bought a round-trip ticket, convinced she would use the return portion soon enough. Fat chance of that. She did not care about economy class, the future, what was or was not going to happen to her. She was happy just to make her escape.

What had she expected of this misadventure? Hadn't she been warned that marrying a *farang* and rushing off to Europe was not quite what it seemed? That it invariably ended badly? That the cultural differences could grow insurmountable? That no amount of money or status was worth the constant irritation, the miscommunications, the frustrations, the loneliness?

She stared out the window as the plane taxied down the runway and felt a surge of relief as the plane took off. Within an hour, tiny Denmark had been left behind.

She did not turn to see who might be seated next to her, did not want to talk, did not want to be bothered, only to savor this precious freedom, this sense of joy now that the burden of these past years had fallen away. She felt like a woman who had come face to face with a tiger in the jungle, had been toyed with for four years, and had lived to see the tiger lose interest and walk away, giving her back her freedom. And just as if she were in a jungle, she kept looking over her (mental) shoulder, expecting to see Martin there, pursuing her, following her, wanting to resume the torment.

Eventually she settled back in her chair and closed her eyes, bored with staring out the window. She was overcome by exhaustion. She was not hungry, not thirsty, not in the mood to talk, to socialize, to read a magazine or to watch television or the in-flight movie. She wanted to close her eyes and forget. So she did.

TWO

IF IT COULD all be traced back, if she could start over, if she could find the moment when it all started to go wrong ... When was that moment? Was it a particular moment or a particular thing? An event? A year? A situation? Where had it gone to hell? When had her karma gone bad? When had her luck changed?

Thoughts of Isa made her heart seize up with a strange, unremitting pain. She wanted to see him, was desperate to see him, had missed him. Was she just being romantic, sentimental? Had Isa come to symbolize the relative innocence of her past, the fact that she had been able to do something right? That, no matter what else she might be—whore, thief, alcoholic—she was also a mother and thus had value and worth, had done what other women could do, was entitled to the respect that all mothers deserved and were so freely given?

Isa. Isa. Isa. Would he even remember her now? The last time she'd seen him, he had been . . . what? nine? ten? Would he care for her now, after all this silence and absence? How old would he be? Fifteen? Would he be working on the banana plantation with her father's men now? Would he have a girlfriend? Would he be taller than she? Filled out? All grown up? Still growing?

Isa. Isa. Isa. She'd done wrong by him. No one needed to tell her that. She should have taken him with her to Bangkok, should have at least said good-bye before leaving for Denmark. But the sight of his sad eyes always stopped her. Those eyes were so sad, so enormously, painfully sad. So capable of accusing her, without a word. So full of happiness to see her, so full of pain when she left. She could not bear it, could not stand to have to look into those accusing eyes and make her parting, could not bear his crying, his whining, his carrying on while his tiny, fierce heart was breaking.

The truth of the matter was that the only person that loved her was Isa. Only Isa would have been sad to see her go, just as only Isa would now be happy to see her again, though at first it might be awkward. Of all the people in her life—the constant stream of men, her mother and father, her relatives, her neighbors, the children she had grown up with—only Isa, her blood, her son, could be counted on. Only Isa loved her truly because she was his mother and he was her son, and there was no breaking that bond, the bond of blood, the unshakable bond of kinship. Isa had crawled out of her womb, and for that, he owed her his life.

She was lonely for him, as only a mother could be lonely for a child. How many men had sucked on her breasts? There was no pleasure in it. But when Isa had nursed, how sweet it had been, how innocent, how pure, how natural. How many men had viewed her only as a sex object, something to be fucked, used, paid, told to leave? Only Isa saw her as a woman, as a mother, as a person.

When she took him into her arms, she would tell him how sorry she was for leaving, how wrong she'd been, how much she had missed him. She had made mistakes. The mistakes were over now. They would go to Bangkok, get away from her parents, live their own lives, be their own people. Her and him. Mom and son. You and me against the world. He would be number one from now on, her first priority. She would make up for all the years, the absences, the tears he had cried. She would make him happy now. It would be just the two of them, somehow or other. She would get a proper job, maybe tend bar instead of working it, maybe scrub the toilets, whatever she had to do. Her free time would be spent with Isa. She would help him finish school. She would be there for him, there in the way that she had not been.

The stewardess brought food. The man sitting next to her—a foreigner, a *farang*—tackled it like it was something to be conquered, something to be devoured. Men were pigs that way, she thought, giving him a secret dirty look. Fucking pigs.

She ate her food slowly, in no hurry, suddenly hungry,

relishing the taste of Thai food. She was on a THAI Airways flight. They were serving chicken with a Thai curry, not one of her favorites, but after so long, it tasted heavenly. She savored each mouthful. There was no hurry. She had time now. No more cooking eggs for Martin. No more lying still for Martin while he humped her. No more ironing his underwear. No more stumbling over stupid Danish words that she could hardly comprehend. No more listening to his tortuous Thai.

The cabin was buzzing with voices and activity. She paid it no mind. Yet it somehow reminded her of home: the banana plantation out in the middle of nowhere. How dark it was at night. Dogs could be heard barking from two miles away. Snakes could he heard slithering through the dry grass. When the winds blew, the banana trees creaked and swayed, their massive leaves producing their own strange symphony, an eerie, disquieting sound.

As a young girl, she had been terrified of those trees, especially at night, terrified of the strange sounds they made, of the snakes that liked to climbed up into them, waiting to drop on an unsuspecting head. Those trees were like ghosts, like tormented lost souls rooted into the dry earth, stuck, imprisoned. Hungry ghosts they were, with tiny little mouths that were always sucking and sucking, trying to get something, anything, to eat, to drink, to suck up, to devour. Hungry ghosts were those who had been uncharitable, who had not given food to monks, who had not made merit during their earthly lives, who had been selfish and stingy and miserly and small. All of those trees were hungry ghosts, she thought, trapped on that abominable plantation, sucking the life out of everyone and everything within their reach. They were sucking, would fasten their tiny mouths on you, would drain you, drop by drop, of the very blood in your veins, if they could. They left the earth sandy and barren. They left the men who worked them dusty and dirty and filled with insatiable lusts. They had left her parents hollowed out, small, stingy, empty.

There was no money to be made in growing fucking banana trees. Anyone with a lick of sense knew that. Her father wouldn't give it up, ignored the signs, pretended that he would be different, that he would succeed when so many others were failing, when their kids were heading off to the city in search of real work offering real money. As she had done.

When she thought of her father, she stopped eating, and there was a pain in her stomach, a long-forgotten pain, a familiar pain that she'd not felt for quite some time now. Her father. Was there a man she could hate more, despise more? Was it possible to hate someone so intensely and not kill that person at the first opportunity that presented itself? Wouldn't a life in jail be perfectly fine just to see a knife buried in that snake's chest? Wouldn't she gladly hang or face a firing squad for the long-overdue pleasure of putting rat poison in his beer and feeding it to him like the "good girl" he had taught her to be?

She pushed the food away now, her appetite gone.

Her father. She hadn't thought about him for so long, hadn't thought about those nights, out in the banana trees, lying in the dirt, terrified of the snakes that might drop on her, in pain because of her father's business driving itself between her legs, humiliated that her father would see her as nothing more than something to be fucked. All men were that way, weren't they? What was a woman, if not something to be fucked? Isn't that how they talked about it? Isn't that what they wanted? Fucking pigs, all of them, her father the worst of the lot.

She was eleven the first time it happened. Her mother had gone away to attend a funeral. Her father refused to go, refused to lose three days of work just to mourn some relative he hardly knew. Her mother had gone, by herself, leaving Nida behind.

That evening, Nida had prepared rice and fish for her father. After dinner, he began drinking. As she prepared for bed, he said he had something to show her, out in the trees. She did not want to go out into the trees; she was terrified of them, afraid they would bend down, grasp her, cling to her, bind her, sucking at her with their tiny mouths. Her father insisted, dragged her, got mean, rude, abusive, used foul language, the sort she'd rarely heard from his lips.

He took her into the trees, forced her to the ground, hiked up her nightshirt. He fucked her. That was what it was: fucking. Not making love. Not even having sex. It was fucking. Animal. Primal. Fucking the way dogs fucked. Shamelessly. Scratching an itch, as Thai men would say. For Nida it was like getting an arm broken or falling out of a tree, or striking her head on the doorway and passing out. It was brutal, painful, hurtful, frightening, too many things to process, to sort out, to comprehend.

He fucked her. Then he left her and stumbled drunkenly back to the house, belching. When he was gone, the darkness seemed even darker, and the trees swayed, and Nida thought they were bending down to grab at her, to get her, to cling to her, to wrap her up in their green arms, desperate to suck at her naked skin with their tiny little horrible mouths.

Was it any wonder that she had stolen money from his wallet to run away when she turned fifteen? That she had bought a one-way bus ticket to Bangkok? Had fallen in with the wrong crowd? Her own bad luck. Bad karma. Fucking bad karma. In her previous life, she must have mistreated her children, so in this life she had been mistreated. In her previous life, she must have cheated on her husband, so in this life she had to make a living by whoring, the ultimate in adultery. In a previous life, she must have taken advantage of someone, and thus in this life she had been taken advantage of by her father, by the mamasans and bar owners, by all those men, by Martin. Four years of marriage to the man, and what did she have to show for it? So much bad karma, pound after pound of it, a whole stinking pile of it, a pile that stunk to high heaven. There had to be an end to it, didn't there? She could turn it around now, couldn't she?

She sighed, turned to look out the window once again. She had been riding the tiger for so long. Tigerriding was glorious, exhilarating, thrilling. The only problem was that when you got tired, you had to get off the tiger's back, and then what? Then you had to either kill the tiger, or be killed by it, if you wanted to be free. If she wanted to live, she was going to have to kill some tigers.

She thought of Isa. She could do it for Isa. Isa would make it worthwhile. Isa would redeem her. Rescue her from her loneliness. Make her believe that her life hadn't been completely pointless, wasted, a meaningless procession of days, an endless series of fucks, an endless stream of men, a constant chipping away at her soul, each man, each event, each situation carrying off just a little bit more of her, leaving her more naked and vulnerable and raw than ever. Isa would make it right.

Isa. Isa. Isa. She had never loved anyone quite so much, had never wanted to see someone so much as she now wanted to see him.

Isa. Isa. Isa. Beautiful Isa. Darling Isa. My boy. My baby. My son. The only thing I ever did right. The only genuinely decent thing I can take credit for.

She fell asleep thinking about tigers and snakes and banana trees and a beautiful little boy with curly hair and gray-green eyes who lit up light a kerosene lamp every time he saw her.

Isa. Isa. Isa.

THREE

Nida Tongwanich did not have the pleasure of killing her father or even just fantasizing about it, because he was already dead.

"When?" she asked, frowning at her mother.

"What's it to you?" her mother shot back.

"Oh, Ma, just tell me when."

"Last year. Heart attack. Out in his fucking banana trees. Got bit by a snake, got panicky. Serves him right."

"So he's dead?"

"Well, obviously."

"And where's Isa?"

"How should I know?"

"Where did he go?"

"He ran off."

"When?"

"Before your father died. It's been about two years, I guess."

"And you didn't try to stop him?"

"Did I try to stop you?"

Nida made a face. All the old resentments, the old hurts, here they were, fresh, like new wounds, like new agonies to endure.

"Well, you know why I ran off."

Her mother pursed her lips, said nothing. She knew. Of course she knew. And after catching her daughter fucking her husband—that's how she thought of idiit was she who had suggested it, who had, in fact, insisted on it. Especially since her daughter was pregnant.

How humiliating it had been. Her own daughter, a whore, her legs spread, lying in the dirt out in the banana trees like a prostitute, letting her father do his nasty business. What a fucking ungrateful bitch. What a piece of trash. What fucking bad karma to have such a thing for a daughter. And what did the bitch do but go to Bangkok and get an abortion, then go to work at a bar called Pussy Glory? Then, after years of this, bring back a bastard child, the offspring of some foreigner, leaving it with her parents so she could go back to her fucking and whoring and money making? Now here she was again.

"I hope you're not planning on staying," she said.

"Where else am I supposed to go?"

"I don't suppose I care."

"It's not my fault he couldn't keep his fucking hands off me!"

"You liked it, and you know it."

"Yeah, right."

"It was your way of getting back at me."

"It was not!"

"You were always lazy, always wanted things the easy way, never wanted to work. You just wanted everything handed to you, like you were some goddess. Please! A whore is more like it."

"He raped me," Nida pointed out. "Ma, I was eleven years old the first time. What was I supposed to do?"

"Like you didn't egg him on, prancing around the way you did. Even then, you were a slut. And you liked it, or you wouldn't have let him do it. Who do you think you're fooling? With my husband, your own fucking father! Haven't you got any shame at all?"

Nida shook her head, not wanting to take up this old argument, exhausted by it. When a woman was raped, it was invariably her own fault. She had dressed inappropriately, had gone somewhere she should not have, had been outside after dark, had left herself vulnerable. That she had done these things meant that, deep down, she wanted it: She was hoping some man would come upon her, would fuck her, would have his way. Even when it happened early, it was merely a tendency already expressing itself, a personality trait already manifesting itself. Every whore, after all, had been eleven once, and there was something in their karma, something in their past lives, that led them inexorably to using sex to make a living. It expressed itself early in some girls. Were they to be pitied for that? For choosing the easy way? Was one expected to feel sorry for them?

Her mother was just as hateful and unforgiving as ever, and she wanted nothing more to do with it. It was old news. It was exhausting, tiresome, odious. Who cared anymore anyway?

SHE LEFT THE house, her footsteps taking her into the banana trees. They had run riot now, as was their tendency. They had to be pruned carefully and kept under control. If not, they spread everywhere, like a disease. She walked into their midst, feeling suddenly small, a little girl again. She heard their moans and whispers, their strange symphony. She thought she could see tiny mouths on their huge green leaves, and she kept well away from them; if one of those leaves so much as rubbed against her shoulder, she would scream. Why had she come back here?

Where had Isa gone? When would her bad karma exhaust itself? What was she to do now?

Isa. Isa. Isa. She had so wanted to see him!

FOUR

TIRED AS SHE was, she did not spend the night, could not stand the thought of sleeping under her mother's roof. Instead, she went back into the village and bought a ticket for the bus back to Bangkok, from whence she'd just come. Had she known Isa wouldn't be here, she would not have bothered at all.

Back in Bangkok, at Pussy Glory, she discovered that Isa had come looking for her, that one of the "girls" had given him some money and told him to go to Lumphini Park. She took a bus to Lumphini Park, but it was night-time and the park was closed. But of course, that was all right. Isa would be one of those boys hanging out, waiting for customers, wouldn't he? What else did those boys at Lumphini Park do, if not whore themselves like everyone else?

SHE CAME ACROSS, quickly enough, Gong and his little gang. She was not frightened of him, not frightened of any man, not frightened of the night. It held no terrors for her, not this concrete jungle, not these particular jackals and wolves and tigers. She was a hard bitch, and any man who looked at her would know as much and beware. A hard bitch would take scissors to your jigly bits and laugh at you while you bled. A hard bitch would outdrink you and leave you to pay the bill. A hard bitch would drug you, let you pass out, steal your wallet, laugh at your stupidity. A hard bitch was not to be messed with because there was really no way of telling just what a hard bitch might do.

From Gong, whom she thought of as a sniveling little weasel whose pecker was probably not more than two inches long, she learned that Isa had once spent some time here but had not been seen for almost a year.

Did any of them know where Isa was?

No.

Had Isa ever been seen?

No.

Honestly?

Honestly.

Isa had vanished off the face of the earth. Isa was not to be found. Isa, when she needed him, was not around.

She walked away from the pathetic little pimp and his little faggy whores, and laughed at the night. Now that she needed him, he was gone. Well, didn't that serve her right? When he needed her, where was she? When he pined away for her, where was she? When he cried into his pillow, sick with his desire to see her, where was she? Now the shoe was on the other foot. Fucking karma. Fucking bad karma.

She laughed at the trees, at the people, the stupid old men looking for sex. She laughed at the cars parked along the street. She laughed at a dog chewing on a coconut husk. Fucking bad karma. You had to laugh. If you didn't, you would throw yourself in front of a bus.

ONE

IT WAS TUESDAY afternoon, and Isa was bent over the desk, the pale skin of his ass cheeks showing, the small, dark hole between them inviting. Khun Jummah had lifted his kurta, had pulled down his pants, had pulled out his erection. He let Isa have it with a sudden jerk of his hips, impaling him, crushing Isa against the desk.

Isa looked at the door to the small school room, which he was supposed to have locked but had not. He was hoping someone would return to the school, would walk in on them, that someone would see, would make the teacher stop. When the pain seized up his lower back, he squeezed his eyes shut, knowing that if he could just get through the first couple of minutes, he would be all right.

For his teacher, Isa was like a drug that he couldn't get enough of. Isa was like candy that one never tired of licking, a drink that left one stumbling about in the dark. Isa was intoxicating, beautiful, capable of giving such pleasure, so submissive, so gentle, so accepting. No matter how hard Jummah might throw his hips forward, Isa never uttered a word of complaint. No matter how many times Jummah made him stay later for "catch-up lessons," Isa never refused.

Isa made him want to fuck. How else to describe it? Not to make love. Not to be gentle and tender and sweet but to fuck. Like a man. To drive his flesh into the body of another, to leave his seed there, to take his satisfactions not like some goddamned pansy but like a real, honest-to-God fucking boots-on man.

The Koran described women as man's "fields," a place where one could "go in" and do what one wished. What Jummah wished was to fuck, and no matter how many times he fucked Isa, he just couldn't find the satisfaction that he was looking for. There was relief, of course, great pleasure, but almost immediately the desire began building up again, and if he could, he would fuck Isa two or three or four times in a row. He was filled with such mad lust that he knew it was sinful, could not be anything but sinful, to desire someone this way, to lust over someone this way, to take such delight in hurting a child. It had to be a sin. It had to be some deep wickedness within him.

How he had prayed to Allah for relief. How he had prayed! And Isa was a child, after all. Of course, he had just turned sixteen, but he was still a child, a student. Someone who looked up to him with respect. Someone who needed his guidance and friendship not his insatiable lust. Why couldn't he stop himself? Why couldn't he get hold of this beast, reign it in, slay it, be done with it?

Every day Isa sat in his classroom, beautiful Isa with his curly hair falling in his eyes, beautiful Isa with his beautiful body, his exotic looks, his come-hither eyes. Oh, the boy drove him crazy. How else to describe it? How could he sit and look at that boy all day long and not want to fuck his brains out? It was just as simple as that.

His life had been fine until Isa had come along. He'd been able to control himself and his desires, only occasionally, when they got the better of him, going over to Lumphini Park to pick up a boy, to bring him home, to fuck him, to get rid of him before anyone saw.

He'd been fine in those days. Had kept things under control. Had not aroused anyone's suspicions. Once a month or so, when his lust got uncontrollable, he indulged himself. Repented. Wept before Allah with genuine tears. Promised to do better, to stop, to obey Allah in this matter, to give up this wicked lust, this terrible perversion.

He was thirty-six now, and all his life he had been fighting this battle. His first boy had not been until he was twenty-nine. Twenty-nine! A virgin until then. But after that first boy, that first fuck, the floodgates flew open, and now he could not get enough. From once every three or four months, to once every month or so, and now every day. And if he could fuck Isa in the morning before classes started, he would do that too.

Why these strange desires? Why did Allah torment him with these unnatural urges? Why hadn't Allah given him the grace to be married and have a family and be normal? Why was Allah testing him in this fashion? Why, when Allah knew how lusty he was, how much he needed sex, yearned for it, longed for it, desired it, took pleasure in it—why had Allah plagued him with these perverted desires for males and the pleasures they were capable of?

He was gripping Isa's kurta now, holding it up so that Isa's back was exposed, thrusting against the boy like a dog in heat, crazy with lust and desire. He couldn't wait for classes to end, for the other students to go away, for sufficient time to pass before they could close up the shutters and lock the door and "do their business." And when they did, it was always over too quickly, and the boy was always too quiet. He wanted Isa to like their encounters, knew the boy did not. He wanted Isa to like him, for that matter, knew the boy did not. This made him suddenly angry. He got rough. He slapped at the bare back. Brought his fist down. Threw his hips forward. Used his knees to spread Isa's legs wider, so wide that it would have to hurt.

Before he wanted it to, his semen erupted, and he was helpless to stop it, helpless in its clutches, and he kept thrusting until his penis softened and slid out of the boys' rectum, exhausted by its master's foolishness. Jummah stood there, panting, staring down at the boy's pale ass cheeks. He felt sorry for the boy now, sorry for what he had done, ashamed of himself. Had he hurt the boy? Had he been too rough? How was he ever going to get the boy to relax and enjoy it?

"You can go," he said, still panting, straightening out his clothes.

Isa very slowly, without turning around, without looking at him, pulled up his pants, let down his kurta, smoothed his clothes out. He walked away from the desk with measured, careful steps, as if he might be in pain. He grabbed his books off a desk and left without saying good-bye.

TWO

"KHUN PAW," ISA said, greeting the Master.

Only Isa used that word, *father*. His sons called the Master "papa," but Isa could not bring himself to employ such familiarity with this man.

"Isa, boy, how was school?"

Isa shrugged.

The Master was sitting in his thinking chair on the porch, a Koran in his lap, an Arabic version. A real Koran, Isa thought. Not a translation but the real words, spoken through the angel to the Prophet Muhammad. God's words. Allah's words. The voice crying out in the darkness and offering a light to man.

"What is it?" the Master asked.

"Khun Paw!" Isa said. He fell to his knees in front of the Master, put his head on the Master's lap, and began to cry.

"Oh, Isa, what's wrong?" the Master asked tenderly, putting his fingers in the boy's curly hair, letting a hand stroke at the back. "Tell your pa what's wrong, eh? You know you can always tell me everything."

But all Isa could do was say "Khun Paw!" again and again. Father! Father! Father! Such pain was inside him now. It wasn't just Jummah and his insatiable lust, although he was growing weary of having to satisfy it. Over the past year with the Master and his family, he had experienced a religious conversion, had come to understand that Allah was real, that Allah loved him, that Allah wanted good things for him—the Master always said so—but Isa was not a good person, never had been. Isa had done such horrible things, such bad things, such impure, immoral things. So while he longed to approach the throne of Allah and seek the mercy of Allah, he was also terrified and ashamed of himself and felt the weight, the burden, of sin upon him, a burden that darkened his days, that left him feeling bleak and despairing.

It was, he thought, the very same way that he felt about the Master. He loved the Master. How could he not? He did! With all his young heart. He wanted desperately to be the Master's son, the way Hamid was, the way Abdul was. He wanted to belong to the Master. He wanted to be able to say, see, here is my father, the Imam, Sheik Ahmad Kloy. This is the man whose blood runs through my veins. This is my protector, my teacher, my father, my kin, my blood. But in the presence of the Master, he felt such great unworthiness, so much so that it kept his tongue tied. He wanted to spill all his life's secrets to the Master, unburden himself, but how could he? How could he tell the Master what he had done? How could he tell the Master about Gong, the gang, the men, the drugs, the liquor, the cigarettes? How could he tell the Master about all the petty thievery, the cheating, the shoplifting? How could he? The Master would be so ashamed of him that Isa wouldn't be able to bear it. The Master would suddenly see that his "Isa, boy" was indeed kaffir trash, the worst of the unbelievers; there was hardly a single bit of wickedness that Isa hadn't stooped to. The Master would be mortified to learn about Isa's past. Embarrassed.

Mrs. Kloy was right. Isa was a snake in the grass, a bad influence. Didn't he and Hamid spend long nights in the sixty-nine position, giving each other forbidden pleasures, while Abdul slept beside them, oblivious? He was a dangerous individual to have around the house, morally corrupt, of bad blood, suffering from bad karma, which he no doubt richly deserved. Nothing was going to redeem Isa from his vices, from his perversions, from the deplorable upbringing he'd been given. No amount of love was going to smooth over these cracks.

"What is it, Isa, boy?" the Master asked, trying to get Isa to stop crying. He was now well and truly alarmed.

"Khun Paw," Isa said, lifting his face, looking up into the Master's beautiful, kind eyes. "If you knew who I was, you would ask me to leave, but I don't want to leave, and I don't want to lie to you anymore. I don't know what to do. I'm so afraid you won't like me anymore."

There. It was said. It was starting to come out.

"Of course you have your secrets," the Master said. "Someday, when you are ready, you will tell me about them, and maybe we can find a way to ease the pain of them. But only when you're ready, Isa, boy. And you know that whatever you tell me, it won't change my feelings for you. You are my son, now. Nothing can change that, Isa, boy. Don't you know that by now? You can say what you will, but you won't change my heart."

Isa had heard the Master say such words on numerous occasions but had never really believed them, could not bring himself to do so. Of course, he was young, and his sins, to him, seemed excessive and overwhelming. Only the young could turn their deeds into such grandiose things.

The Master thought he knew Isa's secrets fairly well, and after many years of counseling men and women—and some children too—he was well aware of how the world could tangle up a soul, how its lusts and passions could overwhelm and disfigure and confuse and terrify. The Master knew that the only way out of this morass was love and forgiveness, generous doses of both. To be human was to be frail, to make mistakes, to choose the wrong path. And for a boy like Isa, without the proper moral guidance during childhood, without someone to look after him, well, what more could be expected? He had been vulnerable, had no doubt been preyed upon, and was now suffering from the things that had been done to him.

Did the Master blame Isa for any of this? Of course not. Isa was not yet old enough to make real choices, informed choices. He was not yet mature enough to stand before Allah and declare his willing disobedience. He had yet to receive the confidence of age that would allow him to knowingly choose the wrong, to knowingly turn his back on Allah, and to thus be fully responsible for the consequences thereof.

The boy had so much to learn. Even so, one had to start somewhere. One had to make a beginning, put down the first tender roots in the hopes of finding nourishing soil. The Master would be that soil for Isa, if the boy would put down his roots.

"What's troubling you?" the Master asked.

Isa had calmed down and was now kneeling on the porch, his arms around the Master's waist, his head on the Master's lap. He was sniffling, still, occasionally reaching up to wipe his eyes.

Over the past year he had filled out and was getting bigger. He was taller than Hamid now. He was, in all respects, a handsome young man. Even Mrs. Kloy was not immune to his charms, to his smile, to his unassuming ways, to his quietness. Even Mrs. Kloy was growing fond of him, though she distrusted him. She had begun to understand that the Master was right: Isa could go either way. He could become a genuine villain, or he might straighten up and fly right.

The dynamic in the house had changed and for the better. Before Isa's arrival, Hamid and Abdul had fought constantly over every little thing. Now Hamid and Isa were like two peas in a pod, inseparable, and they had so much fun together that Hamid no longer spent his days trying to torment his little brother. If anything, it was just the opposite. Hamid and Isa were always receptive to Abdul, always trying to include him. There was no longer the incessant rivalry and animosity.

Mrs. Kloy had, of course, noticed it, and often commented—approvingly—on it. Hamid had changed most of all, she frequently said. The boy was happier now, less given to tantrums and moodiness, less given to tormenting his little brother or making an ass of himself. He seemed genuinely happy, content. It was as if Isa filled some hole in the boy's life or psyche, had somehow completed him.

Having endured four previous ones, Mrs. Kloy knew that teenage boys were nothing if not a pain in the ass. Hamid had been going down that path, but now he had changed. Now he had calmed down. He seemed to have found himself. With Isa around, he gladly helped out: washing the dishes, weeding the gardens, picking mangoes from the tree out back, sweeping the porch, raking up the dead leaves. It was no longer a chore just to get him to do something. On some mornings she was astonished to find Isa and Hamid already outside, picking weeds on their own, just because it needed to be done, not because they had been told to. She never thought she would live to see the day when that boy actually did some chores without having to be told repeatedly.

The Master smiled down at Isa. Like so many other youngsters, Isa knew his own bad habits, his "sins," his misdeeds, but did he know how beautiful he was, how happy he made others, how gentle his disposition, how gracious his acceptance of inconveniences, how genuinely loving and kind his heart was? Of course not. He did not know these things, did not understand their value, gave himself little credit for all his good points, his strengths, his virtues. Love indeed covered a multitude of sins, and Isa's heart was full of love, the most extraordinary love.

"Tell me your secrets, Isa, boy, if it will make you feel better. I don't want to see you crying."

Isa drew back, sat on his haunches, his hands in the Master's lap, his eyes staring at the Master's knees. "I want to become a Muslim," Isa said quietly. "But how can Allah forgive me for what I've done?"

"How could He not?" the Master countered. "Does your teacher think you're ready?"

They'd had this conversation before. The Imam would agree to Isa's conversion but only when Jummah believed that Isa was sufficiently prepared, that he knew the basics of Islam, was familiar with the prayers, understood what was required, and was willing to abide by the consequences of his choice. Only then would the Imam accept Isa's Shahadah, his profession of faith. Only then would Isa be allowed to recite the Kalimah, the words that would make him a Muslim: I testify that there is no god but Allah. I testify that Muhammad is His prophet and His messenger. Only those words, recited in the presence of the Imam and some of the Muslim brothers, would bring Isa into the fold.

"I'm ready," Isa said, emotion in his voice.

"But what does Jummah say?"

Isa dropped his eyes, ashamed. Jummah did not believe he was ready, would not agree to give his permission. Isa suspected that this was because Jummah would have to stop buggering him once Isa became a Muslim. Jummah had said so himself, had said that sexual activity outside of marriage was strictly forbidden, that once Isa had made his profession, he could no longer indulge his shameful passions.

"Maybe you could talk to him," Isa said, lifting his eyes suddenly.

"Of course," the Master said. "Is that what you're going on about, that you want to be a Muslim?"

Isa shrugged. It wasn't, yet it was. He wanted to spill his secrets but could not. "You won't hate me if I tell you ... things?" Isa said quietly.

"Of course not."

Instead of telling the Master anything, Isa got to his feet and slowly walked away.

THREE

"WHY ARE YOU reading that thing?" Hamid asked, nodding his head at the Koran in Isa's hands.

"I like it," Isa said.

"You must be the only one," Hamid replied. He had a history textbook on his knees. They were sitting out by the pond. The light was fading, and soon they would have to go inside.

It was true: Isa liked the Koran. He had been startled by it, shocked even, by this Voice thundering down from Paradise, of how the good would rewarded with "gardens, underneath which rivers flowed" while the evil would be punished with everlasting torments. He had been alternately frightened, aroused, consoled, reassured, filled with doubt. If Paradise and Gehenna were real, where would Isa wind up? Was there even any need for discussion of the matter? Yet the words of the Koran gave him hope that Allah would be merciful, would be forgiving, would be kind, would be compassionate, that for every one step Isa took in Allah's direction, Allah would take ten in his.

He understood now that to be a Muslim meant to be one who submits himself to Allah wholeheartedly, who does not question Allah's words and commands, who seeks to do only that which is pleasing to Allah, refraining from anything dubious or doubtful.

Hamid had grown up with the words of the Koran seared into his mind and memory, his very being. Thus the words no longer meant much to him. He was not coming upon them fresh, as Isa was. He was not sitting and reading them, pages at a time, the way Isa was. He was not getting the cumulative effect that a reading of the Koran could have. He mouthed the words, went through the motions, performed his prayers, did what was required, but his heart was far away from Allah. He believed in Allah because he hadn't yet learned how to do anything else. He believed because it was expected. When it was no longer expected, his beliefs would relax, would be shrugged off like an old coat that no longer fit properly and was of no further value.

Isa, on the other hand, was on fire. Isa believed. Isa had already, in his heart, rendered his submission to Allah, and was only waiting for the Imam to receive his Shahadah to make it official. Isa wanted nothing more than to be a Muslim, to live as a Muslim, to die a Muslim. Islam had given him a way to make sense of his life, something to grasp hold of, a set of values to live by. Isa had been converted, was full of the convert's enthusiasm.

Isa glanced over at Hamid, admiring the young man. They admired each other a great deal. They spent every waking moment together. They spent many nights in each other's arms. Hamid was his brother, his friend, his lover, all wrapped together. Hamid was like the very air he breathed. Hamid gave him all the love his life had thus far denied him, and Hamid drank in all the love Isa could offer and never seemed to weary of it.

They could not know, these two boys, how much trouble a love such as theirs could cause. Had they been male and female, the way these two individuals found and completed each other would have been completely understandable, something to inspire the writing of stories, songs, or novels; something to romanticize. But they were not male and female; they were male and male. Thus there was no glory in their love, only shame and embarrassment. It was not love that moved them but lust, or so it would be claimed. They could build nothing on this love. Rather, if proclaimed, it would destroy them both. This love had no future, not because its participants had grown weary of it but because others could not abide it, would not permit it, would do all in their power to choke the life out of it once it became known.

They did not know any of these things as they sat there, Isa reading the Koran, Hamid studying his history textbook. Had they been told of what awaited, they would not have believed it. And anyway, encased in the sweetness of loving and of being loved, there was no time to ponder what it all could mean, where it was all heading, how it would turn out.

FOUR

AT SCHOOL THE next day, sitting beside Hamid, Isa had trouble concentrating. How badly he wanted to be a Muslim! When he made his profession, the Muslim brothers at the mosque would become his brothers. Muslims all over the world would become his brothers and sisters, his family: a large spiritual religious family, the family of those who submitted to Allah. Just like Hamid, he would be a Muslim. Like the Master, like Abdul, like Muhammad and Bilal, he would be a Muslim. He would be something. He would belong somewhere. He would no longer be rootless, drifting from one thing to the next, with no ties to keep him bound and how willingly he would be bound, if only someone—anyone—could claim him and bind him.

All day Khun Jummah threw glances at Isa, as was his habit, and Isa could read between the lines of those glances, knew what they meant: The teacher was horny.

At the end of the day, the students were dismissed, but Jummah asked Isa to remain behind so that they could continue their "catch-up" lessons.

"See you at home," Isa said to Hamid and Abdul. The two brothers had grown used to Isa staying late at school, waved and made a quick departure. Isa had never told them—or anyone—of what his catch-up lessons consisted.

"Lock the door, if you would," Jummah said, tackling the shutters. Isa pretended to lock the door, again hoping someone would discover them.

With the room closed up, it was hot and sticky and

unpleasant, but there was nowhere else for them to do their business. On occasion they went to the headmaster's small flat, a couple of blocks away, but only on occasion. It would not do for them to be seen together too often, especially going to the teacher's apartment. There would be questions, concerns about undue familiarity.

"I was wondering if you had thought about my becoming a Muslim. Do you think I'm ready?" Isa directed these words at the teacher's back. Jummah turned, frowned, then resumed closing up the shutters.

"Please, sir," Isa said. "I really want to be a Muslim. Am I not ready yet? What else must I learn? You can question me now; I've studied everything, again and again."

"Isa." The word was spoken like an ejaculation, a complaint, a long-suffering sigh.

"Please, sir," Isa said again.

"Isa, I don't think you're ready."

"But why?"

"There's so much you have to learn. You're so far behind. I don't think you understand at all what being a Muslim is about. I don't think you're ready to commit yourself. It's just out of the question right now. Perhaps next year."

Isa's face fell. He could not hide his disappointment, his frustration. He went to his desk and put his books away in his bag.

"We're not finished," Jummah said.

"I don't feel like it today," Isa replied. He was angry, wanted to get away from this man, was tired of this man's excuses. The one thing he desperately wanted in the whole world was in this man's hands, and all he ever got was excuses. Suddenly he could bear it no more.

"Are you angry?" the teacher asked.

Isa said nothing. It would not be polite to admit to being angry, but to say nothing was to admit to it. Yet that was the polite way to do it. So Isa remained silent.

"Is it what you really want?" the teacher asked.

Isa turned to him. There were tears of frustration on his cheeks. He nodded, but didn't dare hope that Jummah had changed his mind.

"Why don't you let me have some time to think about it? I'll talk to the Imam. I'll give you an answer at Friday prayers. Okay?"

Isa relented. Relief swept through him. Was it about to happen, at last?

"It's just that I'm afraid," Jummah said, strangely quiet, strangely humble.

"Sir?"

"I need you," the man said. "I enjoy being with you. You know that, don't you?"

Isa nodded.

"Well, I'm afraid that once you become a Muslim, you won't stay around after school for our extra lessons."

Isa considered this. It was a valid point. It was precisely the point, in fact. Isa didn't want to stay around for their "extra lessons."

"But I was thinking, Isa, that after you become a Muslim, perhaps you should come live with me. We could continue your studies, get you caught up for good. Anyway, I think the Imam and his family must be getting tired of you by now. Haven't you ever thought of that? It's a lot of extra work and money for them to take care of you."

Isa became very still. No one had ever said such a thing to him. The thought of it was a bit shocking. Had he overstayed his welcome? Were they getting tired of him now? Were they just being polite, too afraid to ask him to leave?

"Of course the Imam wouldn't ask you to leave; he's much too polite for that," Jummah said, a look of pity on his face. "But you've got to consider what you're going to do, Isa. You can't impose on them forever, you know. I think it would be much better if you came and stayed with me. I would help you get through school. I'd make sure of that. You could help out to earn your room and board. I'm sure we'd get along just fine."

Isa lowered his eyes. The thought of living with the teacher was not welcome at all. In fact, if he had to go live with the teacher in order to become a Muslim, it wasn't worth it. Nothing would be. He'd rather go back to the streets.

"Now, don't be telling the Imam what I said," Jummah added, his voice earnest. "No need to be upsetting him, and of course he'd just deny it. You know how he is. They've been very good to you, you know. But you shouldn't just take their kindness for granted. And anyway, there's been talk in the community. Mrs. Kloy has been telling people that she doesn't know when you're going to leave, that she feels like she's got another son to take care of. Of course, she tries to pass it off as a joke, but it must be very tiring for her."

Isa's belly seized up with pain, apprehension, embarrassment. He was wearing out his welcome, and Jummah was, in the Thai way, trying to tell him so indirectly, without the main players having to do it themselves. In other words, rather than the Master or Mrs. Kloy taking him aside and telling him it was time to leave, they had started talking to others, and word had gone around the community, and now the teacher was relaying it to him. If Isa had any sense, any self-respect, any "face" at all, he would take the hint.

"I never thought about it," Isa said quietly.

"Well, you should," the teacher replied.

Embarrassed, his face turning red, Isa grabbed his books and left the classroom. He ignored the teacher, who called after him. He was embarrassed, ashamed, had to get away.

Out on the street, the neighborhood looked just as it always did yet somehow suddenly different: exotic, alien, unwelcoming. What were these people saying about him? Was word going around, from the chicken curry shop to the noodle shop to the place where they sold prayer mats to the auto repair center run by the bearded bear of a man, Khun Harun? What were the kids in school saying behind his back? Was Mrs. Kloy going around to her friends, complaining about him, hoping it would get back to him? How embarrassing. Of course, it must take a lot of money to house and feed another person, to pay for school fees, books, pocket money for lunches. Isa helped out around the house so that he could "pay" his way as much as possible, but what good was pulling a few weeds or washing the evening's dirty dishes?

He walked the streets, at first heading for "home" but then letting his footsteps carry him in the opposite direction. It was not his "home." It never had been. He'd been presumptuous to think so. Instead of showing gratitude for their kindness, he had simply taken advantage of it. It was not hard for him to believe that they would be happy if he didn't show up, if he disappeared back into the night from whence he'd come.

Yet he would miss Hamid terribly. He could not imagine life without being with Hamid. He could not comprehend how it would be possible to get through his days. They'd had such happiness being together, living together, sleeping together, sharing their secrets, their hearts, their bodies, sharing everything. He would miss Hamid, and, of course, he could not ask Hamid to go with him. The boy would not survive on the street, did not know how, would not be able to let men take advantage of him, not the way Isa did, not the way Isa was able to. Hamid would be horrified at such a life. Hamid deserved much better. It would break Isa's heart to see the other boy used—mistreated—in that fashion.

HE CONTINUED TO walk, feeling strange now in his kurta and prayer hat. He was a stranger in this place, in this community. He did not belong. It was foolish to think he could become a Muslim, that they would accept him. It did not work that way. Blood was what mattered, and he had no blood here. How could he have forgotten that?

He walked the streets, making a large circle around the Kloy complex. If he went back, he would not be able to leave.

Abdul would be heartbroken. Hamid would be furious. The Master would want to know why. He could not bear the thought of facing them, of telling them he was going to leave. It would be humiliating.

He saw pants and shirts hanging from a window close by, and without thinking, he swiped a set of clothes, already knowing what he had to do. He let his footsteps take him toward the Kloy house. When he found a secluded spot, he changed quickly into the clothes he had stolen. He folded the kurta carefully and put it in his bag, along with the drawstring pants. It was a set that the Master had bought for him, but it would fit Hamid too. Isa could not take any of the Master's things with him, not even the pencil in his book bag.

He reached the gates to the complex when it was dark. He threw the book bag over the gates and hurried off. He did not look over his shoulder, kept his face low, hoping that no one would recognize him.

FIVE

IT WAS QUIET around the dinner table. Without Isa, there was something missing.

"Where is he?" Abdul asked again, for the hundredth time or so it seemed.

"Maybe he went to the teacher's house for dinner," Mrs. Kloy suggested.

"I already went over there. He's not there," Hamid said.

"He's not at school. Jummah hasn't seen him." He picked at his food, upset.

Isa had not shown up at his usual time; he almost always got to the house by five or so. It was now past seven. It was just so unlike him to not come home. They were afraid something had happened to him, that he might have been hit by a car or a bus or something worse.

"We have to do something," Hamid said, turning to his father.

"What do you suggest?" the Master asked.

"I don't know."

"Well, I don't either. He'll probably be along shortly. Probably just got detained somewhere. Let's not make things worse than they are. He's a big boy. He can take care of himself."

Mrs. Kloy was not speaking, was trying to eat while every so often fixing Hamid with a curious stare. She was Hamid's mother, knew her son better than he knew himself, and she knew that there was something going on between Hamid and Isa that wasn't quite normal. Her sons all had friends, of course, very good friends. There had been frequent sleepovers, and campouts, and weekend trips as they got older. Something about Hamid and Isa was different: the way they looked at each other, the way they touched, the way they still showered together, the way she often found them, in the early morning, lying just a bit too close together on their mats, sometimes holding hands, sometimes curled up together. Yet, whatever was going on between them had been something good, something that had helped Hamid to calm down. And she could see very plainly now that Hamid, faced with the possible loss of this strange friend of his, was in for a very rough ride indeed.

She herself had grown fond of Isa and liked to joke with her friends about how she had managed to come up with another son: "seven boys now and still no daughter!" she would exclaim. She meant it, had come to think of Isa as a son: a strange son, a quiet son, a son full of secrets and a sordid past but a son nonetheless. He had always been unfailingly kind to her, respectful, always tried to make himself helpful. She had resented him at first, but that had changed, as the months began to slip away.

"I'm sure he'll turn up," she said, trying to comfort Hamid, trying to sound more confident than she felt.

One of the reasons it had taken her so long to warm up to the boy was because of his manner of arrival. He had come in off the street. A child like that could disappear, back into the street, just as easily. Why get attached? Why let your heart be moved with pity and compassion, when it will just get broken as soon as the child is on his feet and lusting for his old way of life again? Isa wasn't blood, could come and go at will, could disappear without so much as a word. Where would they look to find him?

Unlike her son Hamid, she did not give her affection so easily, was always aware of what could happen, of how things could change.

"It's just not like him," Hamid said, looking gloomy and defeated.

They finished dinner in silence. Still, Isa did not return.

Hamid and Abdul did their schoolwork while Mrs. Kloy cleaned up the kitchen and the Master sat on the porch in his thinking chair. Still, Isa did not come. They all stayed up well past ten in the evening.

No Isa.

ONE

ISA HAD THIRTEEN baht in his pocket, enough for bus fare back to Lumphini Park, enough to take him back to Gong, to the life he had left behind a year ago, a life that seemed impossible to believe, a life he had no wish to return to. Yet, what else was he to do? Where was he to go? Back to his grandparents, the banana plantation, Chok and his friends? Only kin would take him in, and he had no kin, thus nowhere to go, no one to turn to.

He had a seat to himself on the bus, and he sat by the window, astonished by the many houses in the City of Angels. Each house held a family: a mother and father, perhaps with their children; a grandmother too; a grandfather; various cousins, perhaps. The mother's sister and her baby. The father's younger brother, who was having a hard time finding work and needed a place to stay. The permutations were endless.

So many houses: walk-up flats, town houses, cramped apartments, sprawling complexes with three or four small houses in addition to the main house. All these people had a place to call home, a roof over their heads, a place of refuge, retreat. How was it possible in a city of so many hundreds of thousands of homes and apartments and shelters—even poor people had shacks beneath overpasses—that Isa had none to go to?

The houses reminded him of his mother and his father, both of whom were lost to him. Was it fair to say that he had known either one of them? Would he recognize his mother if he saw her now? What to say of his father, whom he'd never seen? If the man picked him up and wanted to have sex with him, how would he know the difference? Or would he somehow know, looking into the man's eyes, that the man was his father? Would they resemble each other? Would some unspoken awareness pass between them, some bit of chemistry, of recognition, of blood recognizing blood?

How ridiculous it all was. Anyway, he was sixteen now and no longer needed his mother and father. He could take care of himself; he'd been doing that all his life. Why should it be any different now? And now, thinking about the two of them, his mother, his father, there were feelings of anger and bitterness. The tenderness, the pining away was gone. Now, if he saw them, he would despise them. He would insult them. He would heap as much scorn on their heads as he could manage. What right did they have to his love, to his longing, to his affection? They had lost that right when they abandoned him. What right did they have to expect him to care about them, to be concerned about their well-being? Had they ever been concerned over his? Oh, if he could see them both now, what he wouldn't say to them! How he would mock them, spit at them, reject them just as forcefully and certainly as they had rejected him.

He pursed his lips together, realizing, even as he thought such things, how stupid they were, how impossible. He would never see his mother or father, would never have a chance to say anything to them, good or bad. That was what hurt the most: the silence. To have such feelings but no one to express them to. To be filled with such hurt but never have the chance to strike back.

His parents' absence said something very clear to him: He was of no consequence. He was not important to them. They did not sit around pining after him. They did not miss him. They did not trouble themselves about him. They had gone on with their lives quite content without him. That was the ugly truth of it: They simply didn't care one way or the other, and he was a fool to think otherwise.

Why this knowledge hurt so much, he was not able to say, but hurt it did. Oh, it hurt. It hurt terribly. It hurt in ways impossible to describe. To know that you had no meaning to your own mother and father hurt so badly that the thought could hardly be entertained. Even puppies in the street were looked after lovingly by their bitch mothers. Even cockroaches had homes to call their own. Even snakes had their nests.

To be rejected by the people who had created you, who

had brought you into the world, by the very ones most responsible for your health and well-being—what sort of atrocity was this? What sort of crime? How had it happened? The traditional answer: bad karma. Was that the truth of it? Isa wondered.

If there really was a God called Allah, why had this God allowed Isa to be born into such misery? What purpose had it served? If the words of the Koran were the very words of God Himself, then what about the ones that said "on no soul does Allah place a burden greater than it can bear"? Was rejection by your own mother and father a burden greater than anyone should have to bear? Why did the Koran speak so lovingly and so often about caring for widows and orphans? Did that apply only to certain widows and certain orphans, those who happened to be born in Muslim communities and to hell with others like Isa and his ilk? If Allah really was "The Most Compassionate, the Most Merciful," where was that compassion, that mercy? Isa could see no evidence of it in his life.

"I hate you," he whispered out the window to himself, to Allah, to his parents, to the houses with their happy inhabitants, to the world that had excluded him. But instead of hating them, instead of letting a feeling of hatred swell up in his heart, he hung his head and let himself cry, ignoring anyone who might see him. What, after all, was "face" when you didn't have one?

TWO

HE REACHED LUMPHINI Park at just after eleven o'clock that evening and was surprised at how little it had changed. Even some of the faces that stared out at him from the shadows as he walked the circumference of the park were familiar, though many were not. It did not take long to find Gong and his friends.

Isa held back, hiding himself behind a tree, full of conflicting emotions. Gong was so familiar to him: his greasy hair, his whiplike body, even the small penis that he had so often sucked. He should be happy to see Gong, a familiar face, a one-time friend, but he was not. He had been down this road before and did not wish to walk it again.

Yet, what else was he to do? Where was he to go? How could he work the park and not run into Gong? And if he paid Gong his one hundred baht per trick, he could count on Gong providing a place to sleep, and food, and even heroin, if he wanted it. Wasn't that something, at least? And wasn't that something better than nothing?

What were the options? There were gay bars, of course, and he could hang around, outside, hoping to pick up horny men after their outings of drinking and dancing. There were brothels where he could easily get a job, his age notwithstanding. In fact, there were some that catered to clientele who preferred young, underage boys. He could easily go to one of them, get a job, put himself under the protection of the mamasan or the "papa"-san, since men usually ran these joints. In exchange for his services, he could count on room and board, a place to stay, someone to look after him.

He hid behind the tree, pondering these options. The thought of the Master struck him with a sudden, almost physical force: the Master, with his white kurta, his prayer hat, his gray-flecked beard, his kind eyes. The Master, whom he had loved like the father he'd never had. The Master whose son he had so wanted to be, had daydreamed of being, had pretended to be. Thinking of Sheik Ahmad Kloy made him seize up inside with . . . what? Grief? Longing? Hope? Despair? Love? Hatred? But it was all so confusing.

This was followed by another sensation: a powerful wave of hatred, hatred for himself, for his own life, for his own bad karma, his own cursed luck. And it was true, genuine hatred, the likes of which can only be generated by someone who has loved first, since hatred is the opposite of love. He had once loved himself, but now he hated himself. Now he cursed himself, his life, his karma, his parents, his circumstances. He hated his body, his paleness, his gray-green eyes, the foreign blood that surged through his veins. He detested that blood. That blood marked him. That blood made it obvious to everyone that Isa was an outsider and did not belong, and would never belong.

Where could he go to escape himself? How could he continue to exist, if not as himself, and what was he to do if that continued existence no longer appealed to him? How could he go on being something he despised so much? How could he hope to be anything different? He could not.

On no soul does Allah place a burden greater than it

can bear—what a lot of crap that was. Filthy fucking crap. *Fuck Allah*, he thought, crouching down behind the tree, his shoulders starting to shake with unwanted tears. Fuck Allah. Fuck the Sheik. Fuck Hamid. Fuck the whole goddamned world.

Had it been possible, he would have gladly allowed the earth to open up and swallow him down. Had it been possible, he would have willed his heart to stop beating, would have willed death to come, would have thrown himself in front of a bus if one was going by.

Of course there is pain in life. To be alive is to be, every once in a while, hurt, or injured, or disappointed, or distressed. What he was feeling was not pain; it was beyond pain. It was such crushing sorrow, such hatred and helplessness and hopelessness that no tears could assuage it, could drain it of its potency. No words could calm his troubled spirit. No god could rescue him from himself. No money, no material thing, could lift him from these depths. The pain of being alive was upon him, and he felt that pain in all its intensity, all its unforgiving disregard.

Oh, for one more night with Hamid! What a strange thought to come to his mind. Hamid, beautiful Hamid, with his warm body, his strong arms, his flat belly, his kind face. To lie naked with the boy, to kiss, to touch, to smile at each other. What sweetness it had been. What joy!

He stood up suddenly, knowing that he could not go back to Gong, that he would not, would rather die, in fact, would rather drown himself in the Chao Phraya River than to start that madness again. What sort of "friend" had Gong been?

What sort of "friend" had he found in heroin? With such friends, why even bother?

He put his back to Gong and started walking, keeping his head low, keeping to the shadows hanging over the sidewalks. Fuck Gong. Fuck the men and their hundred-baht notes. If he died, he would die, but he would not reduce himself to sucking penises again just to scrape by in some miserable existence that he could not stand. Better to die. Better to waste away. Better to commit a crime and go to jail. Better to commit suicide and be done with it than to die that slow, agonizing, humiliating death.

Down the street he went, his footsteps determined, filled with some new energy, some strange strength. He walked all the way down to Rama IV, the main thoroughfare. He turned right, headed for Silom Road, where all the tourists and trendy young folks went to drink and carouse. Further down Silom Road, past the nightspots, the bars and brothels, the Patpong area, with its whores and girly bars, way, way down that street was a mosque, wasn't there? It seems there was. He was sure of it. He didn't know what he would do when he got there, but if he could just make it that far, he could sleep on its steps, could take comfort in its familiar architecture, could hope that a Muslim family in the area might see him, might take him in. Even if no one did, that would be fine; he would wait till morning, attend the early morning prayers, ask the Imam for help: a job cleaning the mosque, perhaps, in exchange for breakfast. Or he could go around the community asking in the noodle shops as to whether anyone needed a waiter or a dishwasher. Better that than these streets. Better that than Gong. Better that than going home to his grandparents.

THREE

AS HE WALKED down Rama IV, past the corner of Lumphini Park where the old whores hung out, he was accosted by a familiar-looking woman who called out his name.

"Isa!"

This woman materialized out of the relative darkness—she had been standing close by the fence—and Isa recognized her at once: his mother.

"Khun Mae?" he said, astonished. *Mother?*

"Oh, Isa!" she exclaimed, hurrying toward him.

When she spread her arms, intending to hug him, Isa backed away. Startled by this rebuff, she too backed away, an uncertain look on her very much aged face.

"Khun Mae," he said again, very quietly, as if to confirm to himself what he was seeing.

"Isa?"

Her appearance was so startling, so unexpected, that Isa did not know what to do. He was literally at a loss for words. So many times he had wondered what this meeting would be like, what he would say if he saw her again. Only that evening, on the bus, he was thinking about how much pleasure he would take in cursing her, in rejecting her, in doing whatever he could to humiliate and embarrass her. Now that she was standing in front of him, he could think of nothing at all to say. When she tried to touch him, he pulled away. When she asked what was wrong with him, he did not answer.

"Of course, you must be angry with me for going away like that," she said, turning her head back and forth to look up and down the street, as if to see who might be witnessing this scene.

"You went to Denmark," Isa said.

"I got married, yes," she replied.

Isa did not press for details.

She bit at her lip, took a deep breath, and stared up at him. He had grown taller than her now. And soon she too was at a loss for words.

"I've missed you," she said.

This earned a curling of the lip that was close to a sneer.

"Really, Isa. I've missed you so terribly. I came down here looking for you; the girls at Pussy Glory said they'd sent you over here, to the park. I want to make it all up to you, Isa. You understand me? I want to make it up to you, make it right. I'm sorry about all of it. You have to believe me."

Isa gazed at her. How unlike Mrs. Kloy she was. Mrs. Kloy would never wear such revealing clothes, would never show off her figure in such a fashion. How old she looked, how small, not at all like he remembered her. She'd gotten heavier, and her makeup seemed garish, her clothes too tight, her voice a bit too frantic. This was his mother? This was the woman he had pined for, had longed for, had missed, had cried over for so many years? This? It seemed like some monstrous, cruel joke.

"Why did you name me 'Isa'?" he asked. That was the fundamental issue, the very beginning of it all: to be named as a silly joke.

She offered a small, uncertain laugh.

"Why?" he pressed, angry with her.

"I thought it would make a nice name. What's wrong with it?"

"You named me after a sign?"

She smiled sheepishly, as if Isa should see the humor in this just as she did. "Don't you miss your mother?" she asked. "I've been back for about a month now, looking everywhere for you. Grandma said you'd run off. I realized you must have gone looking for me. The girls at the bar said you had showed up there. Are you hungry? Let's go eat something."

Feelings of disgust suddenly swept through him, disgust and anger with himself for his own stupidity: He had wasted so much time over this silly woman, and look at her. What could she offer him? He was embarrassed to even be seen with her.

He turned around and walked away. Traffic roared up and down Rama IV, the buses leaving long trails of black smoke behind them. She hurried after him, grabbing his arm.

"Don't you touch me!" he shouted at her, whirling on her, his anger white hot and ready to explode.

"Isa!"

"Fuck you!"

"Isa!"

"You're not my mother!" he exclaimed angrily. "You're a fucking whore. Go fuck someone, why don't you?"

She slapped him.

He said nothing, glared at her, open now in his defiance, uncaring as to what she might say or do. He forgot about the traffic, the cars and buses and motorcycles, the pedestrians, the men walking the street looking for whores like her to take home.

"You're so smart, aren't you?" she asked. "Your mom's just a whore, is she? What do you know? What do you know about anything?"

There was enough of a hint of mystery to these questions that Isa continued to stare at her. People started to gather around them, sensing a fight was about to break out.

"Didn't you ever think to ask yourself why your ma was a whore?" she asked angrily. "You think I just woke up one day and decided to spread my legs? Is that what you think, you stupid child? You want me to tell you about your grandfather, about how he used to take me out into the banana trees and fuck me? Is it time we had a talk about that? Or how your grandmother—Would you like to know how she blamed me and forced me to leave when I was fifteen because my dad got me pregnant? And where was I supposed to go? What was I supposed to do? Are you going to judge me now, you ungrateful bastard? Well, fuck yourself."

"I don't believe you," Isa said.

"I could care less," she replied. "Why should I be surprised? You're just like everyone else. You want to judge me? You want to sneer down your nose at me? Well, fuck you. Fuck all of you. I've had enough of people judging me. What do you know about anything, you snotty little shit? How dare you fucking talk to me like that? Goddamn you!"

She slapped at him again, but this was ineffectual. She turned in a circle, as if dazed. About a dozen people had gathered around them. She glared at each of them, as if defying them with her eyes. She seemed to be coming unglued, disintegrating, unraveling.

"How dare you judge me!" she shouted at the people gathered around. "What the fuck do you know about my life? Who the fuck do you think you are? What the fuck are you staring at?"

She turned back to Isa. "All I wanted was to find you, to take care of you, to make it up to you, and all you do is insult and embarrass me. I should have known there's no end to my bad karma. Just like everyone else, you're going to torment me. Well, we'll see about that, won't we, you fucking selfish shit?"

She pushed her way through the small crowd and headed dangerously close to the road where the buses were whizzing by at terrific speeds not more than a few inches from the curb. If she slipped, if she fell, she could be struck by one of them sooner than she could pick herself up. A horrible sort of screaming erupted from her. It wasn't normal screaming; it was primal. It was anger, despair, hurt, and humiliation—a cry that said no help was wanted because no help would make any difference.

Isa had humiliated her, just as he had wanted, but now he felt bad about it. Now he was questioning himself. Had she spoken the truth? Had her father raped and gotten her pregnant? Had her mother forced her to leave home? Had she taken to prostitution because there had been nothing else for her to do? And hadn't he done the same thing?

Nida Tongwanich lifted her face to the dark sky and uttered a screeching noise that seemed impossible for any human to make. The sound of it was frightening, as if years of hurt and humiliation had piled up and were now spewing out of her mouth in a fantastic display of raw emotion and primal rage. Isa, embarrassed by this display of emotion, turned around and walked quickly away, losing himself in the crowd.

FOUR

ISA WALKED AIMLESSLY. Traffic picked up at two A.M., when the bars closed. Multitudes of taxis swept past with drunken passengers in the backseats. Motorbikes, cars, limos, more buses. The young, the trendy, the beautiful, the foreigners, all wandered the streets, and dogs too, looking for scraps, something to eat, anything a vendor might have dropped or left behind, and up and down Silom Road shoppers were outnumbered by vendors selling everything from noodles to pirated copies of CDs and movies, not to mention cheap T-shirts and porn videos.

Isa, who'd not eaten since lunch that day, was not hungry. His feet hurt from so much walking, but he could think of nothing else to do, nothing else he wanted to do but keep walking, as if his walking could help him to find something that would comfort him, or at least bring some warmth to the coldness in his belly and the ache in his heart. The hatred he felt for his mother was so visceral and unexpected that he wasn't quite certain what to make of it.

On Silom, down past the gaggle of vendors and drunks and bar goers and bargain hunters, Isa found himself being followed by a tall Thai man dressed in expensive clothes. He looked to be about fifty years of age, still fit, still handsome. Yet there was something of the shark in his eyes, something that said he knew what he wanted and had enough money to purchase it. The man eventually drew alongside him.

"I should like to take you home," he said. "What would that cost me?"

Isa glanced sideways at this man, understood instinctively the type of man he was, and said nothing. This was a man used to buying whatever he wanted, who was without shame, who was beyond the reach of the law, whose wealth had given him every advantage and no disadvantage. Isa had come across these types before. They usually wanted something more substantial than a blow job. They were into S&M, or pretend games. They liked to be tied up. They liked to wear uniforms. Or they liked their boys to wear uniforms: dresses, women's underwear, men's underwear, a schoolboy's outfit, a schoolgirl's. These were men with exotic, highly refined tastes.

"I'm not in the mood," Isa said. That was true.

"I'll make it worth your while."

"I just want to sleep."

"So sleep then. When you wake up, you might be more agreeable."

"You have to let me sleep first."

"Fine."

They walked on in silence.

"What's your name?" the man asked, seemingly content to follow and in no hurry to close the deal.

"Hamid," Isa said, lying. "My name is Hamid Kloy."

"That's a strange name."

"I'm a Muslim."

"Are you indeed?" the man replied, as if making a joke. "Are you headed in any particular direction, or should we go back to my car?"

Isa stopped, turned, shrugged his shoulders. Then he followed as the man led him back the way they had come.

In the car, Isa got a good look at this man. He had a goatee, looked sort of arty, like an artsy-fartsy fairy. Yet he did not talk like one. He talked like a man, a straight man.

The car, a BMW, had a luxurious smell and feel to it. The man said nothing as the expensive vehicle plied the streets, pulled up to an apartment complex, and then passed by the security guards. They walked into a well-appointed lobby and took the elevator to the twentieth floor, where the man had a penthouse.

Never had Isa seen such wealth. Somehow it seemed empty, silly, stupid. He was not impressed by it. He wanted to sleep. If the man killed him during his sleep, so much the better. If, after he woke and showered, he decided to stiff the man and leave without doing anything, what difference would it make?

The man had a king-size bed. Isa flopped down on it, not so much as bothering to remove his shirt and pants, or rather, the clothes he had stolen earlier that evening. The man protested and undressed Isa. Isa paid no mind. Naked, he let the man put a comforter over him. The man sat beside him on the bed. Isa felt so exhausted, so sad, that he began crying softly into his hands. The man did nothing but rub Isa's back and tell him to go to sleep.

FIVE

ARUN JURASAK WAS a lawyer who had inherited a substantial fortune from his father, had lived a life of ease and plenty, and, despite all that, was tortured by demons he could never quite conquer. One of those demons was his love for men. Given his social position and the status his wealth conferred, he was not free to indulge himself in just any old fashion. He had been forced into the respectable route: marriage, a family, the outward appearances of normalcy and legitimacy. To have done less would have been to risk his family's reputation—its face—and thus would have been impossible. He could not bring disgrace on his respectable family just because he longed for a man to give him a blow job.

His attraction for others of his gender went back, way back, as far back as he could remember. Even in grade school, he had nursed crushes on the "cute" boys, had entertained vague, erotic notions about them. In his late teens, he began to experiment. By his early twenties, he was a frequent patron of discos and watering holes catering to gay clientele.

Throughout his years abroad, earning his degree in law, he had continued to explore. By the time he had returned, degree in hand, ready to join a prominent, high-powered law office, he had already had sex with close to four hundred boys and men.

Denying his homosexuality was not possible. Pretending otherwise, though, was another matter. When the family proposed a marriage to a young lady from a family equal in wealth and status, he allowed himself to be swept up in it. He did not want to marry any woman, but marry he had to, so what difference did it make whether it was this girl or some other girl? He would do what was required. He would father children. He would provide for his wife and children. But his heart would always be elsewhere. And indeed, it had been.

For the first decade of his marriage, he was so busy with work and small children around the house, that he hardly noticed the time going by. Then the unease began to settle in, the realization that he had chosen wrongly and that there was nothing that could now be done about it. He could not divorce his wife, could not walk away from his children, could not abandon what he had started. He had made his bed and would have to lie in it. So he allowed himself to be carried along, to continue the charade. He kept his secrets to himself, though a few close friends were well aware of his proclivities. He honored his marriage vows, as much as possible, though, on occasion, he was not above visiting certain establishments where the young men would take you upstairs for an hour or two of love-making. He always tipped generously and treated them with the utmost courtesy and respect.

There were other demons, though, and now that he was fifty years old, those demons occupied more and more of his time. Time—that was the worst of them. Time was slipping away, never to be recovered. His body kept changing, kept getting older. He could see it, in the lines of his face, in the sag of his belly, in the yellowing of his teeth, in the slowness of his walk. Time was marching on. He was getting older with each day, and soon, like all others who have walked the earth, he would die.

He no longer thought so much about sex, had come to regard sex as something for young people, a sort of toy that one eventually grew bored of and put away. Though sex had once consumed him, now it hardly crossed his mind. There was, after all, so much more to life than reproductive urges.

Never a religious man, he had lately taken to reading dharma books, trying to understand the strange suffering that had come upon him, the strange fears that filled him, the unease that kept him awake at night, prowling about his expensively furnished apartment. He had three mansions as well but rarely spent time with his family anymore.

So much wealth he'd been given, but happiness had been elusive. A beautiful wife, four wonderful, very dear children—two girls and two boys—who were turning into wonderful, very dear adults. His wife had been kind, had never troubled him, had accepted his distance and coldness with grace and resignation. His family life had given him nothing to complain of. His career had been exceptionally lucrative. There wasn't a luxury or honor that hadn't been piled on top of him, regardless of the fact that most of the clients he defended were guilty as sin and everyone knew it. But they were rich, and that was that.

All of it was so meaningless now, so devoid of comfort. His wealth and status were, in so many ways, a curse. There was no end to the claims made upon him for time, for money, for charity, for employment, for a recommendation, for advice, for consultation, for partnering, for golf games/dinners/social events/charity galas/birthday parties/ribbon-cutting ceremonies... On and on it went, never giving him a moment's peace. He employed a "social secretary" just to keep on top of his social life, not to mention a personal assistant and three office secretaries. He would gladly give away all his wealth if people would stop making demands on his time, because time was the one thing that he had so precious little of now, and time was the thing that was slipping away from him, slipping through his fingers, forever lost and irretrievable.

What did he have to show for it now? A marriage, four children, a successful career, a fat bank account, but so what. Happiness—real, genuine happiness—had been elusive. He had never found the completeness of being in love with another being like himself. Had never lost himself in the charms of a beloved. Had never experienced that heady pleasure of delight and ecstasy. Had never awoken in the morning to find his beloved asleep next to him. Had never awoken to find his beloved caressing him or pleasuring him or offering him breakfast in bed. Had never let himself be so loved by a man that he would be willing to let that man fuck him, invade him in that primal, savage fashion. He had chosen the status quo, the safe route and was now reaping the rewards or lack thereof.

The more he read dharma books and reflected on his life, the more he realized how right the Lord Buddha was, that there is suffering, that we bring it upon ourselves, that our cravings and desires are bottomless, endless, that, if we let them, such cravings will drive us into madness, loneliness, despair.

He had lived a selfish life, had done well for himself, but what difference had his life made to anyone else? There was so much misery and poverty around him. What had he done to relieve it? There were boys without fathers, girls without mothers, children without homes. How had he helped them, he who had so much wealth he didn't know what to do with it? He had benefited from a system that kept the rich rich and the poor poor. What had he returned to society in token of his gratitude? What sort of works would follow him into his next life? What sort of merit had he made? Good merit? Bad merit? Wealth was supposed to be an indication of his good karma, his good fortune: that he had earned a great deal of merit in his previous life and was now enjoying its rewards. But why did this wealth seem so oppressive, so empty, so meaningless, so much a burden? Why did the monks prowling the streets at six in the morning seem far happier than he was?

Sex had been a demon. Time. Regrets. A disillusionment with the world. Questions about the point and purpose of his life. All this swirled about in his head, never giving him rest. And as the months and years went by, the questions, the unease did not lesson, but only increased. Death was pressing in. If he didn't solve these riddles, he would die and be none the wiser for having lived, and to him that seemed a waste indeed. If he could not find some peace in his mind, what was the point of living?

It was six in the morning now, and sunlight was streaming over the horizon. He had a fantastic view from his twentieth-floor apartment windows. The boy he'd brought home the night before was still in his bed, oblivious to the world, sleeping as if he might never have the chance to sleep again. Arun sat down on the bed, looked at the boy, admiring his youthful muscles, his curly dark hair, his air of innocence. To be young again. To know what he knew, but to be young, to have the chance to do it over . . .

From the look of him, this boy was not a street boy. He did not wear the sort of clothes that street boys—money boys—wore. He did not have the unhealthy, malnourished, glassy-eyed appearance that most had. He was obviously new, in from the provinces. He did not look as if he belonged to the creatures of the night who prowled Bangkok's dirty, congested streets and alleys. He looked like a boy who was quite out of his depth.

The boy had said his named was Hamid Kloy. An unusual name, Kloy was. Not a name one usually heard. He was a Muslim. It should not be a difficult matter to track down the boy's parents, see them reunited. He could have his secretary call around to the mosques, see if the Kloy family could be found.

He smiled as he looked at the boy. "Hamid" was beautiful,

had a life stretching out in front of him, had the benefits of youth and grace and strength, all the things that Arun no longer had. Still, he could be happy for the boy. Could do something to help him. Could treat him the way he would wish to be treated, if their positions were reversed, if he had run away from home in some fit of youthful stupidity or angst. He could not go back and live his own life again, but he could help others, couldn't he? Especially youngsters, young gay boys who needed guidance, protection, love, and not simply to be taken advantage of because it was so easy to do, so easy but ultimately so unsatisfying.

After watching the boy for many minutes, watching the rise and fall of his chest, the beautiful curve that the boy's body made beneath the coverings, he got up and went to his windows. The sun was out in force. A new day had arrived, and each new day held the promise that something new and different could happen. And, Arun thought, perhaps it might.

10

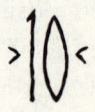

ONE

THAT MORNING, AFTER prayers at the mosque, the real Hamid Kloy went out to the pond in the back of the house He climbed up into the mango tree, retrieved his smoking supplies, and made himself a cigarette with a banana-leaf wrapper. He smoked it, trying to find comfort in it but could not.

It was Thursday, the last day of the school week. He should be preparing for school. He'd told his mother he didn't feel well and wasn't going. She had merely shrugged.

For an hour or more, he sat there, staring at the placid waters of the small pond, plucking grass, tossing it aside, drawing puffs on his makeshift cigarette, feeling generally miserable and out of sorts. He missed Isa. That and something more. Without Isa, life seemed empty. It had never seemed that way before, not until Isa had come along. Isa had made everything different. Now he did not know how he was going to carry on, how he was going to survive. Without Isa around, he didn't want to. School seemed unimportant. Eating, sleeping, talking—it all seemed useless and boring and trivial. Without Isa, his world was black and white, all the color gone, all the joy and vividness, the vibrancy, the happiness, all of it gone.

He knew very well what the truth was. How could he bring himself to say it, to admit it to himself, much less to anyone else? He loved Isa. Like a boy mooning over a girl. Like the sweethearts in the stupid soap operas. Like his father grinning while he swatted his wife's behind. He was in love with Isa, in love with a boy, not a girl. They had never spoken of it, the two of them, had never said what was in their hearts. Hamid could sense that the other boy returned his affection but was not sure. Now, with Isa gone, he would never know.

And it wasn't like there could ever be anyone else like Isa or that he could ever feel this way about anyone else. At sixteen, with hormones whirling around in his bloodstream, he did not think it possible that his heartbreak could feel any worse, that it could ever be relieved, that he could ever live again. He did not believe anyone else in the world could possibly understand what he was feeling; if they said they did, they were just lying. No one else could know what he felt, how much it hurt, how crushing the weight of it was.

He rolled another cigarette. At this rate, he would develop a smoker's cough. He decided he didn't care.

TWO

KHUN JUMMAH—AS a teacher, that title of respect, Khun, Mister, was always put in front of his name, whether deserved or not—viewed the absence of the Kloy boys with some alarm. Last night, Hamid had come round, inquiring if Isa had been seen. Apparently, after their conversation in the schoolroom, Isa had not gone home.

At prayers that morning, Jummah had learned that Isa was gone, nowhere to be found or seen. Now his students were arranged in orderly rows in front of him, but Hamid and Isa were missing. Hamid had been at prayers that morning, but hadn't looked well, not at all, and Jummah thought he knew what that meant.

Like Mrs. Kloy, he had seen Hamid and Isa together, had seen the way they looked at each other, they way they carried on. There was something more there than friendship, Jummah was sure of it, and if there was, then no wonder Isa was not interested in leaving the Kloy home and coming to live with him. This realization made him angry. Jealous.

Taking in Isa had become an obsession. To have the boy around, underfoot, sharing an apartment—what he wouldn't do! His mind conjured up all sorts of erotic fantasies concerning showers, the single bed, what they would do in the morning before school, what they might do on their days off, the life they might live together. He could be like Isa's bigger brother, taking care of him, taking his pleasures in return, and who would know the difference?

The more he had thought about it, the more he was

obsessed by the idea, frantically casting about for a way to make it happen. Yesterday he had made his move: He had told Isa that the Kloys were getting tired of him.

That was not true. Mrs. Kloy had indeed been telling her friends that Isa was just like another son, but she had been doing that in a jesting, secretly happy sort of way. She was growing fond of him, was proud of him, was proud to have him about, wanted others to know that Isa was now part of her family.

Jummah knew that it didn't take much to tip the balance, not when face was involved. Most folks would do most anything to avoid a loss of face, and he had judged rightly: Isa had been so embarrassed that his first thought had been to leave. That was the Thai way. When you realized that you had overreached or had worn out your welcome, you immediately moved on. The Thai way also involved friends and associates pointing out these things so that the principal players would not have to.

After making his move, Jummah had then trotted out the idea that Isa should live with him, believing that Isa would jump at the chance, would jump at this face-saving measure, but the boy hadn't, and his plan had gone astray. The boy had run off altogether, which Jummah hadn't at all expected.

Now he was in a pickle. If Isa showed up and told the Imam and his family what he had said, Jummah would be in trouble. If the Imam found out about their after-class "lessons," Jummah would be in trouble. In fact, Isa was nothing but trouble, and perhaps his leaving was best for all concerned. And of course, if Isa had left, Jummah knew where to find him.

THREE

SHEIK AHMAD KLOY, after leading the noon prayers at the mosque, took Khun Jummah aside.

"Have you seen Isa?" the old man asked.

Jummah shook his head. "I thought he was sick today or something." That was a lie but delivered smoothly and with complete sincerity.

"He didn't come home last night," the Master said.

"Really?" He feigned ignorance, indifference.

"You don't have any idea where he might be?"

"I wouldn't know," Jummah said easily. "I don't really know the boy that well."

The Master pursed his lips. That was a habit of his. It was suggestive of many things: skepticism, disbelief, uncertainty. He trained his watery brown eyes on Jummah but said nothing.

Jummah, sensing an opportunity, said, "You know, there's something I've been meaning to tell you."

The Master raised his eyebrows.

"Yes," Jummah said. "Isa and your boy, Hamid, . . . Well, they seem very fond of each other, don't they? Maybe a little too fond? And I caught them once, doing . . . Well, I would rather not say. I suppose you know what I mean."

The Master continued to gaze at him, not speaking, his eyes full of questions and doubts. Jummah felt suddenly nervous. Did the Master know something? Suspect something? One could never tell, not with Sheik Ahmad: he always seemed to know things that he had no right to know. It was as though he could see straight through you, straight through your lies.

"I just thought you should know," Jummah added. "Isa was asking me again about becoming a Muslim and, well, what can I say? To be doing the things that the Prophet Lut's people did, the people of Sodom . . . Well, I've been stalling. I suppose you can understand why. I just don't know what to tell him. And of course, to be involving your son in such things. Well, it's troubling. Don't you agree?"

The Imam did not reply.

"If you'll excuse me," Jummah said, in a hurry to get back to his students, to get away from those accusing eyes. Let the old man make of that what he would.

FOUR

THE MASTER WALKED home slowly, his heart filled with questions. Bitterness was in his steps and not a little anger. He was aware of this, made no effort to indulge it. Feelings sometimes came of their own and left just as swiftly.

He was attached to Isa, and now the Beloved had separated them. The Beloved was jealous, of course. Not that the Beloved resented any affection that Ahmad Kloy might lavish on an orphan boy, but, rather, the Beloved wanted the Imam to keep his priorities straight. It was the Beloved's business to "save" Isa, not the Imam's. It was the Beloved who would work out all things, in good time, not the Imam. It was the Beloved who was the Sustainer and Creator of the universe, the soul's best and dearest friend, the highest and purest good.

You must do as You please, Sheik Ahmad thought, directing his thoughts to Allah. *Nothing can happen, but that You will it.*

It could be that Isa was now gone from his life. If that was the case—if he had rendered the service that Allah had desired, and his part in the matter was now complete—then so be it. He wished Isa well. He prayed that the Beloved would watch over the boy, would fulfill His purposes for the boy, would bring him safely to the fold of Islam, in whatever fashion the Beloved deemed best.

It was hard to offer these sentiments, because he wanted to be the one who received Isa into the Muslim community. He wanted to be the one who helped Isa, who kept the boy around, who served as a substitute father. He could not help himself. Compassion had gotten the better of him. His heart had gone out to the boy. He was a sentimental old fart, that was certainly true. Over the past year, he had come to love the boy, to think of him as his own, as a sweet and dear son who he hoped would always be around.

The temptation was there: to give in to feelings of bitterness. To question the Beloved. To even curse the Beloved for this turn of events. He fought the temptation, forced himself to renew his submission to Allah, his "Islam"; among other things, "Islam" meant submission. He would submit to Allah, even if his heart cried out against it. He was merely the creature. Allah was the Creator. Allah knew best. Surely that was true.

At home, he was informed by Mrs. Kloy that Hamid was out back, sitting by the pond, and had refused to come in for lunch. The Imam let his feet take him in that direction, and he found his second youngest son sitting at the foot of the mango tree, smoking.

With a guilty look, the boy tossed the cigarette into the pond.

"Papa," he said, standing up, wiping at his mouth, as if he could wipe away the smell of the tobacco.

"Smoking, are you?" the Imam asked but not unkindly. It wasn't exactly a secret, though Hamid thought it was. The Master had learned long ago that letting his children explore the darker bits of the world on their own—and making a few mistakes too, while they were at it—was the best way to teach them.

Hamid, sensing that he wasn't going to be scolded, visibly relaxed.

"Do they taste good?" the Imam asked.

"Papa?"

"The cigarettes?"

Hamid made a face.

"So why do you smoke them?"

Hamid shrugged.

"If your mother catches you, she'll wash your mouth out with soap, you know."

Hamid made another face.

"Your mother says you won't eat."

Hamid sat down, turning his troubled gaze back to the waters of the pond. He did not respond.

"Do you want to tell me about it, about you and Isa?"

Hamid glanced up sharply, alarm in his eyes.

It wasn't that the Master didn't know about that business, either. The Master knew just about everything that went on in his house, of course, and if he had been really bothered by it, he would have intervened. Like the smoking, Hamid would undoubtedly grow out of it, would move on to other things or perhaps not. But the boy was of age and could make decisions on his own.

"Well?" the Master pressed.

Hamid shrugged.

"You miss him?" the Imam asked.

Hamid nodded.

"You love him?"

Hamid did not answer.

"It's not wrong to love someone," the Master said.

"You don't understand," Hamid said. That was one of his stock phrases. Like most teenagers, he was convinced that no one in the world had ever felt the way he did, or had experienced the things he was experiencing.

Instead of talking, the Master took a seat next to his son and put an arm around the boy's shoulders, as if to say that he did understand, and indeed he did.

FIVE

WHEN ISA WOKE up, it was well past four in the afternoon, and the lavish apartment was utterly still, its owner nowhere to be seen. He sat up slowly, for some reason surprised to still be alive. So much had happened yesterday that his mind just couldn't process it all, but now he felt better and worse. He thought of his mother, and his heart seized up with grief. Why had he walked off like that? How was he to find her now? Or would they run into each other at Lumphini Park while they both trolled for tricks? He thought about Hamid, and felt a different sort of grief. He had grown used to waking up and seeing the boy there, on his mat, right beside him.

He got up and dressed quickly. The stillness was disorienting—it was never quiet in Bangkok—and he had a phobia about being alone: Nothing bad happened to you, not unless you were alone. Had the man simply left him sleeping while he'd gone to work or wherever? The thought of it made him afraid.

He looked out the windows in the living room, the view somewhat astonishing. He could see the Chao Phraya River in the background, a host of skyscrapers marching away in all directions. In the bathroom, he found a note taped to the mirror.

Esteemed Hamid Kloy,
I had to leave you. My apologies. Work to do, all of that.
Please feel free to help yourself to anything you like. There's plenty of food in the kitchen. You may order room service; the restaurant downstairs does great chicken dishes, though I don't recommend their seafood. Stay, if you wish, or leave. Feel free to steal anything you like. I could honestly care less. You would be doing me a favor, getting rid of some of this junk I've collected. You probably wouldn't believe how boring it has

become to me. So please feel free to take whatever you like, if you're so inclined. I shant miss any of it in the slightest.

I have a variety of engagements, won't be home till very late. If I see you then, we shall discuss your future. If not, perhaps we shall see each other again sometime.

You will find, in the drawer by the fridge in the kitchen, an envelope with some money, should you need it. I've also left a cell phone there, with my private number programmed into it: Just call "A" if you want to reach me.

Do you need a friend, Hamid Kloy? Give me a reason, and we shall see.

Sincerely,
Arun Jurasak

Isa read this strange missive three times, trying to decide if he understood it. Steal the man's things? Money? A cell phone? He rushed from the bathroom to the kitchen, looking for the drawer, and found it. In the envelope was fifty thousand baht, more than one thousand American dollars. It was more money than he had ever seen in his entire lifetime. It was a fortune.

He read the letter again, frowning:

Do you need a friend, Hamid Kloy? Give me a reason, and we shall see.

SIX

THE NEXT TIME he woke up, he found the man sitting on the bed, watching him. Self-consciously, he sat up, rubbing at his eyes. It was dark. The clock on the nightstand said it was past midnight.

"I must have fallen asleep," Isa said, sheepishly.

"Must have," the man agreed.

"I forgot your name," Isa admitted.

"You never asked," the man replied.

"Sorry."

"Don't be sorry. My name is Arun. How are you feeling, Hamid Kloy?"

"My name's not Hamid," Isa said.

"I know that. I was wondering if you did."

"Excuse me?"

"Your name is Isa Kloy, from what I understand. You are the son of Sheik Ahmad Kloy. You have apparently wandered away from home, for reasons which I could not even begin to guess at."

"How do you know all that?"

"You can compliment my personal assistant, should you ever meet her. She can do wonders, you know. Anyway, I'm a lawyer. We get paid to know things."

They regarded each other warily.

Isa was wondering when the man would want to have sex. That's all they wanted, really. That was the bottom line.

"So what should I do with you?" Arun asked.

Isa didn't know.

"Why didn't you take my money and leave?"

"I don't want your money," Isa replied. That wasn't quite true, but he had enough pride and self-respect not to just steal it. If need be, he would "pay" for it by rendering the services required.

"Well, then, I suppose you should go," Arun said, standing up.

He was wearing silk pajamas, and, despite his age, he was not unattractive.

"I don't understand," Isa said. "What do you want from me?"

"I don't want anything from you," the man replied.

"Don't you want to have sex?"

"Don't be crude."

"I don't get it."

"Would you really like to know what I want?" the man asked, turning around to gaze at him, a strange sort of longing in his eyes.

Isa said nothing, waited for the man to continue.

"I want to be you," the man replied.

Isa frowned.

"I want to be young. I want to do it all over again. You wouldn't understand that, but that's the truth. Rather stupid of me, I know, but there you are. I've excelled at not being stupid, and look where it got me."

Isa glanced around the apartment, not quite grasping this point. It seemed to have gotten him very far indeed.

"What are you doing, Isa, running away? What do you hope to find out here? Are you being mistreated at home?"

"Of course not."

"Then why did you run away?"

"Because it's not my home. I'm not related to them; I was just living with them. How do you know about this anyway?"

"I talked to Sheik Ahmad. Seems to be a fine fellow. He was surprised that you'd run off, couldn't imagine why or where you'd gone."

Isa frowned and lowered his eyes.

"It really wasn't hard. 'Kloy' is an unusual name, and as soon as we started calling around, we figured out that Sheik Ahmad Kloy was probably the man we were looking for. Are you hungry? Should we order some food and talk?"

"I don't understand what it is you want from me."

"To help? Is that a crime? Or would you prefer that I just took advantage of you and kicked your sorry ass out on the street? Is that it? Fuck and run, all that?"

Isa didn't know how to respond to this.

"Are you hungry?" the man asked.

Isa nodded.

The man went to the phone and ordered room service. Isa went to the bathroom, closing the door behind him, feeling very much out of his depth. He wasn't afraid of the man; unless he was very much mistaken, the man had no intentions of hurting him. It was just that talking to him was confusing.

In the living room, he sat down on the sofa while the man claimed the easy chair. These items were placed in front of the windows, offering a view of the Bangkok skyline at night. A million lights lit up the night.

"Do you have a family?" the man asked, folding his hands together, looking, somehow or other, very official, as if he were conducting an interview with a potential client.

Isa shrugged.

"Care to tell me about it?"

"Why?"

"Perhaps I can help. I didn't get to be as old as I am by being completely stupid. And I remember what it was like to be young: How I wished I had listened to my heart!"

Isa didn't know how to proceed, so he said nothing.

"Tell me about your mother, your father," the man prompted.

In halting tones, with long embarrassed pauses here and there, Isa told the man his story. By the time he was finished, their food had arrived, and they had spread it out on the coffee table, eating while they talked. For reasons he didn't understand, Isa told the man everything, absolutely everything. Partly it was bitterness and hurt, and partly a need to tell someone his secrets, to have it all out, every last ugly bit of it. He told the man about his grandparents, about the banana plantation, about Chok and the men, about going to Bangkok, about his mother, her absence, about Gong, about being found by the Master. He told him about Hamid, what they did together, how much he liked it. He told him about Jummah. Everything tumbled out of his mouth, and he was helpless to stop it.

Afterward, as they finished up their meal, the man sat back in his easy chair and closed his eyes, as if meditating. Isa, having said so much, was now embarrassed. Never before had he told someone his life story, not even Hamid.

"So what are you going to do now?" the man asked, at last opening his eyes and regarding Isa carefully.

"I don't know," Isa said honestly.

"Then you won't mind if I offer some suggestions."

> 11 <

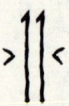

ONE

KHUN JUMMAH WAS surprised to see Isa show up at the school, at just after three thirty P.M. on the following Monday, after the afternoon prayers had been said and all the students had left. Isa opened the door to the boys' classroom and walked inside, offering a small, uncertain smile.

"Isa?"

Isa greeted the man respectfully.

"Where have you been?" Jummah demanded in an angry tone of voice. "The Imam's been looking for you. How could you go off like that?"

"I was embarrassed," Isa said quietly. "Because of what you said, that they didn't want me around anymore. Anyway, I was wondering if you would let me stay with you."

The teacher regarded Isa with flat, unreadable eyes.

"Please?" Isa added.

"Actually, I think it's best if you just stayed away."

"I want to be a Muslim," Isa said. "I'll do whatever you say. Just let me be a Muslim. Tell the Imam I'm ready. I can go live with you, couldn't I?"

Jummah, sitting at his teacher's desk, considered this proposal.

"But I don't want to have sex with you anymore," Isa added. "It's not right."

"Not right?" Jummah repeated, raising his eyebrows.

"You shouldn't be taking advantage of me," Isa said. "You have no right to make me do those things."

"Is that a fact?" Jummah asked, standing up.

Isa nodded.

"So, some kaffir piece of trash is going to tell me what's right and what's not? Is that it?"

"I just want to be a Muslim."

"I think you should leave this community and not come back."

"But I want to be a Muslim."

"Who cares what you want? You think this community wants some heroin-addicted little whore running around and having sex with everybody?"

"I was not having sex with everybody."

"I know about you and Hamid."

"I can do what I want."

"So it's all right for you to have sex with him but not with me?"

"I don't want to have sex with you," Isa said. "You have no right to make me."

"If you want to be a Muslim, you'll do what I say!"

"That's not fair."

"I think you should leave," Jummah said.

"I'm going to go talk to the Imam," Isa said defiantly. "I'm going to tell him that I'm sorry for being a burden to him, that I didn't realize what I was doing. I want to thank him for helping me."

"That's not a good idea."

"It's only right that I say good-bye. They might be worried about me."

"They're not worried about you. I talked to the Imam this morning, and he said he was glad that you were gone, though of course he would never tell you that."

"I don't believe you."

"Believe what you like, but it's the truth. Now I suggest you leave this community and don't come back."

"And what if I go tell the Imam that you used to pick me up in the park? What about that?"

"He won't believe you."

"Yes he will. He knows I've never lied to him."

"No one will believe you, Isa. I'll just deny it anyway, and you're not going to say a word about what we did, not to the Imam, not to anyone."

"And why not?"

"Because I'll kill you."

"So you're threatening me?"

Jummah came around the desk but then stopped, giving Isa a sideways glance, as if his body wanted to do one thing, his mind another.

"I won't say anything," Isa said soothingly. "I just want to be a Muslim. Let me stay with you. I don't care about having sex. If you like it, we can do it. But just let me stay. I'm scared, out there, by myself. Just let me stay with you, and I won't tell anyone anything."

"I'll never be able to trust you," Jummah said.

"We only had sex a few times," Isa said dismissively.

"We had sex every single day!" Jummah exclaimed loudly. Then he looked around, as if he realized he was speaking too loudly. "I'll never be able to trust you. Just leave now, Isa, if you know what's best for you. And don't come back around here again."

"But where am I supposed to go?"

"What difference does it make? Who cares? Just go!"

"But where? I don't have anywhere to go. Please, I'll do anything you want, just don't make me go."

Isa went around the classroom, closing up the shutters, as he once used to do. Though he hadn't planned on them, tears had sprung to his eyes. He went to the door, pretending to lock it, then turned to look at Jummah.

"Please?" he said quietly. "I'll do anything you want. It doesn't matter to me. Just don't make me go. If I stayed with you, I could finish my school. I could get a job, pay you back for taking care of me. Please?"

Jummah went back behind his desk and sat down on his wooden chair. Isa approached the desk slowly, not looking at the man. Instead, he turned around, presenting his backside, lifting up his shirt so that the man could see his back. Jummah put a hand on Isa's buttocks, rubbing them through the fabric of his jeans. Isa undid the jeans, allowed the man to push them down, to expose the flesh beneath them.

Isa cried silently as he did this, could not comprehend why. He was filled with such shame that it was like a physical thing. He felt embarrassed for the teacher to be looking at him, looking at his private parts, yet he had never felt embarrassed before. What was going on now? What was the difference?

Jummah forced Isa's jeans down until they were tangled about his ankles. Then he stood, lifting the front of his kurta, ready to do his business, the temptation too much to resist. Isa squeezed his eyes shut when the pain erupted in his backside. He cried out for the man to stop.

Jummah did not.

"Please!" Isa exclaimed, trying to twist away. "Stop it!"

"You shut up!" Jummah shot back. "If you want to stay with me, you better get used to it."

Isa continued to struggle and cry out, when the door to the classroom suddenly banged open. In walked Sheik Ahmad Kloy and three of his six sons: Hamid, Bilal, and Muhammad. Following was another man, an older Thai man who was very expensively dressed. And coming in behind that man were two more: police officers in brown uniforms.

Jummah sat back down on his chair abruptly, forgetting all about Isa, about the sex, the pleasure, the mad lust inside him. He hurriedly put his business away, smoothing over the front of his kurta, staring at these intruders with uncomprehending eyes.

The expensively dressed man came forward. "Well, well, well," he said agreeably. "What do you know about this?"

TWO

ISA IMMEDIATELY BENT down to grasp his jeans, pulling them up, embarrassed that the others should have to see him this way. Hamid hurried across the room to help him and lead him away, with a reassuring arm over Isa's shoulders. Isa was made to sit down, and Bilal and Muhammad immediately converged on him, kissing him, touching him, reassuring him with their presence, with their love.

"Isa?" Arun said, holding out his hand.

Isa undid the top button of his shirt, then removed a tiny tape recorder that had been hanging from a chain around his neck. He handed it to Arun.

"I think we have enough," Arun said, turning to face Jummah.

"Who the hell are you?" Jummah asked.

"Isa's lawyer. Imagine that!"

"His lawyer?"

"Oh, indeed."

Jummah was flabbergasted.

"And rather than Isa leaving, I believe—it's merely my opinion, mind you—that you should be the one to leave. A teacher who routinely abuses his students is not what this community needs. Wouldn't you agree?"

Arun turned, as if he were in a courtroom, looking from the Imam to the police officers. There was nervousness all the way around. Only Arun seemed at ease. The police officers were plainly embarrassed to have been dragged into the middle of something so delicate. The Imam had a pained, uncomfortable look on his face. Jummah, of course, had reason to be nervous.

"How could you lie to this boy?" the Imam asked, approaching the desk now. A sudden resolve had come over him. "How could you tell him that he wasn't wanted at our house? Have you no shame? Where was he supposed to go?"

"I never said that," Jummah replied.

"You're a liar," Arun pointed out. "And we all just stood outside this door listening to you repeat it. The words you used were, if I remember correctly, 'I talked to the Imam this morning, and he said he was glad that you were gone, though of course he would never tell you that.' Isn't that what you just said? It's on this tape recording. Shall I play it back? Refresh your memory?"

Jummah licked his lips, that very telling bit of body language that signals guilt and uncertainty.

"And how could you abuse him?" the Imam asked, approaching the desk more closely. "He's a child, for heaven's sake! What sort of animal are you? Allah brought this child into our midst so that we could help him, not take advantage of him. I've known you all your life, Jummah. I'm surprised at you. Disappointed. How could you do this?"

Jummah, this personal note being added to the conversation, now seemed to pale.

"I must ask you to resign," the Imam said.

"Of course," Jummah said, not lifting his eyes to look at the man.

"I am prepared to keep my mouth shut," the Imam added, "as long as you do the same."

Jummah glanced up.

"Isa has his secrets," the Imam said quietly. "We know that. You know that. Now, so do you. You keep your mouth shut. We'll keep our mouths shut. "

The teacher looked around, from the Imam to the lawyer, to Isa, to the Kloy boys.

"What's done is done," the Imam said. "The past is past. What we are trying to do is build a future for this boy. He wants to be a Muslim. So be it. You have no right to stand in his way. You have no right to try to scare him away or make him feel that he's not worthy of being a Muslim or that he isn't wanted in this community."

A long silence ensued.

Jummah struggled with his emotions, his embarrassment at having been caught, the realization that what he'd been doing was hurtful and wrong, which he, of course, knew very well, and always had.

Isa, with Hamid sitting next to him, calmed down. With the Kloy boys around, he felt stronger, calmer, more sure of himself.

"Do you admit to molesting this boy?" Arun asked suddenly, turning his gaze on Jummah.

Almost imperceptibly, Jummah nodded.

"Are you aware of what could happen if word got out about this?" Arun pressed.

Jummah did not respond.

"I will hold on to this tape recording," Arun said. "You've had a close call. If I were you, I would try not to make it any worse. I would pack my things and move on. Then again, if you'd like to play with someone your own age, I feel more than up to it. If you ever lay a hand on this boy again, I'll make certain you live long enough to regret it. Am I making myself clear?"

Jummah said nothing, only stared at the floor in front of him.

"Is it settled then?" Arun asked, looking around the room.

There were nods. Nothing would be said about Jummah as long as the man resigned his position as headmaster and left the community.

"Then I'll supervise while the good teacher cleans out his desk," Arun said, offering Isa a smile. "The rest of you needn't bother. Why don't you take Isa home?"

"Yes, of course," the Imam said. "I can't thank you enough."

"You needn't thank me at all," the man replied.

THREE

OUTSIDE, IN THE familiar street, with the Kloy boys standing beside him, Isa felt such incredible happiness sweep through him that he thought he was in the midst of a dream.

Arun came through the door, fixing his keen eyes on Isa, smiling.

"I don't understand," Isa said to the man. "Why did you help me?"

"Perhaps I shall explain it to you sometime."

"No, please," Isa said. "Why? I really don't understand you."

The man took his arm and drew him aside where they could

talk privately. "We don't belong in this world, do we, Isa?"

Isa frowned.

"You will see, as you get older, what I'm talking about. You and me, we're not like other people. We will never fit into their world, no matter how much we try. Look at me: I got married, had kids, did everything I was supposed to do, but I don't fit in anywhere. I have no home, not really. The only time I feel any sort of connection with this world, with the people of this world, is when I'm with someone like you, Isa, someone who's like me, who understands what I've been through, how lonely it is. We're outsiders, Isa. If we don't take care of each other, who's going to do it?"

Isa considered this in silence. Like so much else that the man had said over the past several days that they had been together, it made little sense. It sort of did, but then it didn't, not really. At least not in any way that made sense to him.

As if reading this thought, the man said, "Someday, you'll understand."

"Well, thank you anyway."

"I should thank you," the man replied. "This whole escapade has been very exciting for me, if you only knew! Much more exciting than dinners with senators and their boring wives. I may have to do it again sometime."

Isa smiled.

"Stay in touch, Isa," Arun said. "You'll be hearing from me again. I've decided to pay your way to college if you get good grades."

"You can't do that," Isa said, somewhat embarrassed.

"I can and I will."

FOUR

"HOW COULD YOU just leave like that?" Hamid demanded.

Hamid and Isa were out back, near the pond, smoking banana cigarettes. Isa did not reply. What was there to say?

"Don't ever do that again," Hamid added.

"I'm sorry."

"Sorry's not enough. You scared me to death."

"Well, you know." What else was there to say?

"Maybe it's wrong, but there's been something I've been meaning to tell you."

"What?" Isa inquired.

"It's kind of hard to say." There was a look of intense earnestness on the boy's face.

"What?"

"I sort of love you. You know. I didn't realize that until you were gone."

Isa smiled. "I sort of love you too. You know."

They smiled at each other. The awkward moment passed. And as for what the future might hold for them, they did not care, not in that moment. The future would reveal itself soon enough.

FIVE

ISA SAT ON the floor of the mosque. He was surrounded by the Kloy family: Hamid, of course, and Abdul but also

Muhammad, Bilal, Ahmed, Sulay, the Imam, and several friends from school.

"Now," the Imam said, "since you've demonstrated that you know what Islam is, what its teachings are, how to live the Islamic life, I want you to repeat after me. We'll do it first in Arabic. Okay?"

Isa nodded.

The Imam led him through the Shahadah: I testify that there is no god but Allah. I testify that Muhammad is His slave and His messenger.

With those words, said in Arabic, repeated in Thai, Isa become one of those who submit themselves to Allah, one of the world's billion-plus Muslims.

Isa grinned foolishly. A great weight fell off his shoulders. His belly felt fluttery. He had found a home, a place where he belonged, a safe place where he could bloom and grow.

The Imam beamed. Hamid beamed. All agreed that Isa, in his kurta and kufi, looked like he had been a Muslim all his life.

Isa was so overcome with happiness, he broke into tears, but they were happy tears, tears of relief, of joy, of, for once in his life, belonging.

He was to have many other adventures, but that's another story altogether.